I ♥ Band!

by Michelle Schusterman

Grosset & Dunlap
An Imprint of Penguin Group (USA) LLC

GROSSET & DUNLAP
Published by the Penguin Group
Penguin Group (USA) LLC, 375 Hudson Street, New York, New York 10014, USA

USA | Canada | UK | Ireland | Australia | New Zealand | India | South Africa | China

penguin.com
A Penguin Random House Company

Cover illustration by Genevieve Kote.

Library of Congress Cataloging-in-Publication Data is available.

ISBN 978-0-448-45683-6 10 9 8 7 6 5 4 3 2 1

For the geeks,
band or otherwise

Sometimes being a perfectionist just isn't worth the effort.

I spent the entire last week of summer break preparing for my first day of seventh grade. I made a band practice schedule and stuck to it—three new minor scales, plus I memorized the school fight song (it's the only music I had that I knew we'd be playing in advanced band).

For my other classes, I made lists. And charts. Color-coded ones—this was serious stuff. I printed out a map of Millican Middle School and drew in the routes for all of my classes, including locker stops and bathroom breaks, in red. Then I took my best friend Julia's schedule and drew her route in purple (two classes together, lunch, and two potential bathroom meet-ups if she can make it to B-hall from English in less than a minute).

It took me four hours to choose an outfit. Normally

I don't take *that* long, but the first day of seventh grade is a big deal, right? I ended up picking one that coordinated with the new backpack Mom got me—light blue with red zippers and straps. The blue-and-white-striped shirt and denim skirt were hanging on my closet door handle. My red hoodie, too—Texas summers are hot, but the schools are *frigid*. Got to prepare for AC overload.

See? Totally planned out. And it took my dumb troll of a brother about two seconds to screw it all up.

"Chad!"

I stared down in disbelief. Orange juice soaked my shirt, my skirt, and the sad excuse for a napkin on my lap. Across the table, Chad's eyes widened. Then he did what any dumb sixteen-year-old guy would do after once again ruining his little sister's life—he laughed.

(Really, it was more like a snorty-grunt noise. Total troll, I swear.)

"Chad, it's not *funny*! Do you have any idea how long—?"

"Holly, honey." Mom grabbed the nearly empty carton and handed me a towel. "It was an accident."

"I know," I said through gritted teeth, picking up the wet orange lump that had been a napkin and tossing it onto the table. "He slept late, ran down here a minute before we have to leave, tried to eat breakfast even though he doesn't have *time*, and spilled juice all over me because he had to rush. And because he's a troll."

"Holly," Mom said warningly, wiping the juice that was dripping off the table. Chad grinned, which was particularly gross because he had, like, an entire chocolate muffin in his mouth.

"Whatever." I stood up. "I have to change. Maybe that red top and jeans will go with my—" I glanced down at my backpack between my chair and my French horn case and shrieked.

"What now?" Mom sounded exasperated. I pointed a shaking finger at my bag, soaking up all the juice that was still trickling off the table, and she winced. "Oh dear."

She picked it up. The entire front was stained an ugly dark orange color. Chad snickered again.

"It looks like someone puked on it. Aaand here comes the freak-out," he added when I closed my eyes.

I once heard the phrase "apoplectic with rage" used to describe being so angry you might actually physically explode. Thanks to my brother, I totally understood what that meant.

"Chad." I clenched my fists (which were all sticky from the juice, which only increased my apoplecticness). "I swear, you are—"

"Holly, stop." Mom glanced at her watch. "Chad, apologize."

He rolled his eyes. "Sorry." (At least, that's what it sounded like. About half a muffin fell out of his mouth when he said it.)

"But, Mom—"

"Holly, we're already late," she interrupted. "You need to change, I need to find another bag you can use, and Chad needs to brush his teeth—seriously, that's gross," she added when he grinned again. "Everybody move, now."

I stormed up the stairs and to my room, wondering if Dad would start taking me to school if I got up at five every morning.

Staring into my closet, I did a quick mental assessment. My entire clothes timeline was ruined. The red top wouldn't work because tomorrow's outfit was red. The pink-and-brown-striped shirt was scheduled for Friday. Yellow dress? A little *too* dressy for the first day; I'd look like I was trying too hard . . .

"Holly, just *pick something*!" Mom hollered from down the hall.

"Fine!" I hollered back. "It's not like this is important or anything!"

Two minutes later I walked into the dump Chad called a bedroom wearing the yellow dress, the red hoodie, and the biggest scowl I could manage. Mom was on her hands and knees, rummaging through his closet (and somehow not suffocating from the dirty sock stench).

"What are you doing?"

"We donated your old backpacks a month ago, remember?" Her voice was muffled.

"Yeah, and Chad's, too," I reminded her.

"Right—but I'm hoping we missed one. You know

how hard it is to find stuff in here. He never throws anything away."

"Mom, I don't want to use one of Chad's nasty old bags!" I cried. "Can't we just—"

"Just what?" Mom straightened up and gave me her deal-with-it face. "Holly, we donated *all* of your old school stuff. It's either one of his old backpacks or a shopping bag. Your choice."

"Stellar," I said, glaring at her. She stood on tiptoe, her navy high heels wobbling a little bit, and felt around the closet's top shelf.

"He definitely gave me the bag he used last year, but you know Chad . . . he probably didn't look around too hard for any other—*aha!*" Mom pulled down something black with straps and waved it at me triumphantly.

"Mom. Look at it."

She turned it over. Her face fell when she saw what was printed on the back. "Well, that's . . . that's not so bad."

"*Mom.*" She had to be joking. "I'm not going to my first day of seventh grade with a *Batman backpack.*"

Mom nodded slowly. "Okay, fine. So, paper or plastic?"

Apoplectic. Yeah, I so totally got that word.

We were late for school. Okay, not *late* late, but I would barely have time to find my locker—or Julia—before first period. And of course we had to drop off Chad first, just because the stupid high school was closer. And my backpack was only a tiny bit less humiliating than a grocery bag.

By the time we pulled up to Millican, I was about five seconds away from a stroke.

"Haveagreatdayloveyoubye!" Mom waved out the window as I raced up to the entrance, horn case in hand, the ridiculous bag with its obnoxiously bright yellow Bat-Signal shining like the ultimate Beacon of Nerdiness on my back. Too late, I realized my dress was yellow, too. I'd coordinated my first-day-of-school outfit with a nine-year-old boy's backpack. Stellar.

According to my watch (which was still perfectly set to the school's clocks, down to the second), I had just over two minutes before the warning bell. If I hurried, I could still drop my horn case off in the band hall and find Julia at her locker.

Less than a minute of talking might not seem worth it, but I hadn't seen Julia in almost a month. Her family always spent the last two weeks of summer at the beach. And before that, she'd been at Lake Lindon Band Camp.

When I'd come home with the brochures for Lake Lindon on the last day of sixth grade, Mom and Dad promised me that I could go the summer before I started high school. Julia and I had geeked out over it together—cabins, swimming, a big concert, *and* a dance. Daily rehearsals, too. Every minute of every day was scheduled.

Total heaven.

We were both shocked when we found out Julia's parents were sending her as a surprise present for her birthday in July. I mean, I was happy for her. (And a little jealous, but how could I not be? There I was, practicing my horn every morning all by myself in my room with Chad banging on the wall, and Julia was getting to eat, sleep, and breathe band every single day with a bunch of other kids.)

Her parents picked her up after camp and went straight to the beach house they shared with her aunt and uncle and a bunch of cousins. We got to talk on the phone some, but Julia was always really busy with family stuff down there. So the last month of summer break was pretty blah without her. No wonder I was so ready to be back at school.

The halls were swarming. I apologized to about a zillion kids for whacking their knees with my horn case before I made it to the band hall. The director's office was empty, but I noticed something written on the chalkboard:

Leave your instrument against the wall. Be sure it has a name tag.

A long line of cases stretched around the perimeter of the room. I added mine (it already had a name tag, of course), and noticed a clarinet case with a familiar purple tag that read JULIA GORDON. Grinning, I hurried back out into the chaos.

Mrs. Wendell had retired at the end of last year. She was awesome—at the spring concert, she gave me the "Outstanding Sixth-Grade Musician" award. Plus she always let me help with making concert programs and fun stuff like that.

My schedule just said "Dante" next to "Band," so I didn't know if the new director would be a guy or girl. My stomach fluttered nervously, although I didn't really know why—I practiced a *ton* this summer. Rounding a corner, I wondered what Mrs. Wendell told the new director about me. I mean, about all the band members. But especially the ones that got awards.

Something to speculate about with Julia, if I could find her.

I made it to C-hall and saw her at the end of a row of green lockers. "Julia!" I yelled, not caring how dorky I sounded. I waved frantically, trying to get around a cluster of wide-eyed sixth-graders. "Julia!"

She was laughing too hard to hear me. Laughing at something some girl was saying. I'd never seen her before, but I noticed one thing right away—she had a light blue backpack with red zippers and straps and no orange juice stains.

I slowed down a little bit. Who *was* this girl? She smiled, flipping her dark brown, shiny hair over her shoulder, whispering something to Julia. Julia whispered something back, and they both giggled.

"Julia!" I waved, moving a bit faster now.

She still didn't hear me. Closing her locker, Julia linked arms with this girl and they started walking toward me, heads close together, still giggling. They looked like they'd been best friends for years. They looked like Julia and I usually looked.

Yeah. Seventh grade was off to a great start.

I stopped dead in the middle of the hall. A sixth-grader bumped into me and I gave him a look that probably made him want to run screaming back to elementary school.

"Julia."

She looked up (uh, *finally*), and her eyes widened. *"Holly!"*

We squealed and ran toward each other and hugged and made a big stupid scene because that is exactly what you're supposed do when you haven't seen your *real* best friend in a month. I glanced at the new girl over Julia's shoulder. She was smiling, but giving me the Eye. The same one I'd been giving her a minute ago.

Good. All was right with the universe again.

"You're *late*! I can't believe Holly Mead was actually *not* at school half an hour before the bell on the first day!" Julia shook my arm, beaming. "I'm so sorry I didn't call you back yesterday, but—"

"I called you *three times*!" I exclaimed. "What on earth were you doing?"

"We got home so late Saturday night, there was a lot of back-to-school stuff to do—you know how my dad is—and last night I was—"

"She was setting a world record for most pieces of pizza ever eaten in one sitting," the new girl interrupted with a grin, and Julia cracked up. I kept a smile pasted on my face, but my stomach dropped. Hang on—she was hanging out with *this girl* last night?

"Sorry, what am I doing?" Julia said, still giggling. She pulled the girl forward. "Holly, this is Natasha. We met at Lake Lindon."

Oh.

"Oh," I said. "Um . . . hi."

"So good to finally meet you," she said. "Julia told me so much about you!"

Oh my God, this girl was such a phony. I could already tell.

But I just smiled and hoped it looked more genuine then hers. "So, um . . . where are you from?"

"Georgetown. My mom got transferred, so we moved here in June," Natasha replied, flipping her hair over her shoulder. Again. "I was *so* excited when I found out Julia goes here, too! We practically lived together at band camp. Cabin sisters!"

Oh.

"That's why I was hanging out with Natasha last

night," Julia said quickly. "She called because they screwed up her schedule, and she—"

The warning bell rang. I forced another grin.

"Don't worry about it. So . . . history, right?" I had Julia's schedule memorized.

"Yeah," she said, adjusting the barrette holding her curly black hair out of her eyes. "See you fourth period?"

"Yup. Nice to meet you," I lied to Natasha, unzipping my backpack and groping for my schedule to double-check the room number.

"You too. And that's a, um . . . really cool bag, by the way." Natasha giggled, and I felt my face burn.

Ugh—Batman. I'd totally forgotten.

"Yeah, it's a long story," I said lightly, and Julia grinned at me. "Anyway. Have fun in history." Wow, I could not have said anything more lame.

"We will!" Natasha linked arms with Julia again, and with a wave, they headed down the hall.

So they had first period together. That figured.

If the orange-juice disaster hadn't been enough, this Natasha girl showing up completely threw me off my game. My English teacher called my name at least three times before Gabby Flores poked me in the back and I finally raised my hand. Then in third period, the PE coach said, "Carrie Leed?" and I was all, "Here!" like an idiot.

I was a little distracted.

Understandable, considering what a mess the day had turned into.

I could not believe Julia spent the last day of summer break with some girl she barely knew and didn't even *call* me. Two weeks of camp together was maybe enough to become pretty good friends, but Julia and I went back to second-grade music class. I mean, we rocked the Owl Creek Elementary talent show with a recorder duet of "Nobody Likes Me." It ended with us tossing gummy worms into the crowd. We got third place.

How could anyone not be best friends for life after that?

And the other thing that was bugging me: I really, *really* wanted to go to Lake Lindon. I'd been okay with waiting a few summers, but that was before Julia got to go. I should have been there, too. We should have been in a cabin together, going to rehearsals together, the dance, the concert, everything.

But instead, she'd done all of that with Natasha.

Plus, Julia and I had both been placed in the advanced band for this year! That was kind of a big deal, since that band was mostly eighth-graders. Keeping up was going to be hard enough—band camp probably would have helped me a lot.

It wasn't like I'd been doing anything better stuck at home—mostly just practicing, watching movies, and trying to avoid my brother's idiot friends. And if I'd been at band camp, Julia wouldn't have had to resort to hanging out with that stuck-up Natasha girl. Who had my backpack.

I kicked the Beacon of Nerdiness under my desk and sighed.

It was a long wait until fourth period band. I mostly spent it imagining forcing Natasha and Chad to eat actual worms.

Chapter Three

I forgot about the new band director until I got to the band hall and saw him leaning against his office door, watching everyone. It was obvious he was a lot younger than Mrs. Wendell, but she was so nice, and he looked . . . not mean, exactly. But maybe a little intimidating.

The message on the chalkboard from this morning had been replaced:

Backpacks in your cubby, instruments out. Please sit in your section.

Underneath that was a seating chart with each of the sections labeled. Organization. I approved.

The cases that lined the wall this morning were gone, too. I headed to the cubby room, mumbling a few hellos. Julia and I weren't the only seventh-graders in advanced band, but there weren't too many of us. Gabby waved at me as she hooked the neck strap to her saxophone. Next to her, Sophie Wheeler was putting her oboe together and talking a mile a minute. I recognized Trevor Wells opening his trombone case and talking to Owen Reynolds, who'd been in my beginner French horn class. Owen's really nice, although honestly, I was kind of surprised he'd been placed in this band. He was an okay horn player, but not great or anything.

No Julia yet.

I found the horn cubbies and noticed they were all newly labeled with everyone's name. So clearly this Mr. Dante was a perfectionist, too. Score one point for the new guy. I slid my case out of its cubby and crouched down on the floor to open it. More kids were filing in—most of them eighth-graders—and I kept my eyes fixed on my horn as a sudden wave of nervousness hit me. This was a whole lot more intimidating than beginner French horn class.

I straightened up to put my case away, horn in hand, and someone's elbow collided with my head. I rubbed my temple and turned to find myself looking into the most insanely dark brown eyes I'd ever seen.

Well, hello there.

That's not what I said, though. What I said was something more like, "*Mermph?*" Because I'm cool like that.

"Sorry!" Aaron Cook gave me an apologetic smile. I couldn't move. It wasn't my fault—he had pretty much the most amazing smile ever. It was paralyzing.

"Um, it's okay." *Seriously, Julia, where are you?!* I watched Aaron open his trumpet case and tried to come up with something at least a little bit not lame to say. But all I could think about was the pep rally last year when Julia and I sat huddled on the bleachers together and discussed the wonder that is Aaron Cook in a football uniform.

Football—maybe I could ask him about that! Was he on the eighth-grade football team this year? Probably. What position? Running back. Wow. How cool. Yup, I was having an imaginary conversation in my head with the guy standing right next to me.

He put his case away and glanced at the floor. "Is that yours, Holly?"

I recognized my blue polishing cloth lying next to my backpack. Bat-Signal facing up. Of. Course.

"Yeah, thanks." I ducked down, grabbed the cloth, then moved to block the backpack from him. Like he hadn't already noticed it. Tucking the cloth back into my case, I realized something. "How did you know my name?"

It just kind of blurted out of my mouth without permission, and I blushed. Aaron grinned and tapped the label on my cubby.

HOLLY MEAD

Oh, for the love . . .

"Right." I wondered exactly what shade of red my face was now. Any hope of me saying more than two words that weren't completely idiotic was dashed when Aaron spotted a few of his friends. "See you!" He smiled at me again—*help!*—and walked off. I watched him go, because let's face it, at that point I already looked like a total loser. I figured I might as well embrace it.

"Excuse me."

I stepped aside as someone reached into the cubby under mine and pulled out a French horn case. The label over the cubby caught my eye.

NATASHA PRYNNE.

No.

No *way*.

I stood there dumbly as she straightened up and gave me that fake smile. "Hi, Holly!"

"Hey." I tried to smile back, then picked up my backpack and crammed it into my cubby before she could say anything rude about it (again). "So . . . you play French horn, too?"

I tried not to sound as annoyed as I felt. How had I not seen this coming? Natasha and Julia were at *band* camp together—duh, of course she's in band. And as if that wasn't bad enough, did she have to play the same instrument as me? *Really?*

"Yeah. Julia told me you're really good," Natasha added. I shrugged, but in my head I was, like, *You got that right*.

Something occurred to me as we headed into the band hall. "So how'd you get into advanced band?" I asked casually. "We all had to audition at the end of last year."

"I auditioned at my old school, too," she replied. "They put me in the top band there, so . . ."

"That's great," I said. *Not really*.

Julia was already seated, clarinet pieces in her lap and reed in her mouth. She waved at me. (Okay, at us.)

I waved back, then slipped past Natasha down the third row and grabbed the first chair in the horn section, right next to the saxes. The bell rang, and everyone hurried to their seats. Brooke Dennis sat down on my left—she'd been the only seventh-grade horn player in advanced band last year, I remembered. Owen sat next to her, so Natasha was stuck with the last chair in our section, farthest from me. Good.

Gabby sat down on my right. "Hey again, Holly!"

"Hi! Have a good summer?" I asked.

She shrugged. "Kind of boring. Want one?" She rattled an open box of Red Hots at me, and I shook my head.

"No, thanks."

"I've got the last lunch period," Gabby complained, shoving a few into her mouth. "Still have PE after this, and I'm already starving."

Before I could reply, the new guy stepped onto the podium. Everyone stopped talking.

"Hello, everyone," he said. "I'm Mr. Dante. Welcome to advanced band."

Silence. (Except for Gabby chewing.)

"I'd like to go over a few rules. Several of you were in this band last year, some of you were in symphonic band as seventh-graders, and a few of you were just beginners. No matter what class you were in, this year might be a little bit different than what you're used to."

Gabby popped a few more Red Hots into her mouth. Mr. Dante smiled at her.

"Let's make this rule number one, Ms. Flores," he said. "No food or drinks during rehearsal."

"Even if I have to wait till last lunch?" she asked. A few kids laughed.

Mr. Dante nodded. "Afraid so." Gabby closed the box and tucked it under her chair with a sigh.

He went over a few more rules, none of them any different than Mrs. Wendell's—no playing without permission, no playing each other's instruments, have your instrument out and be in your seat by the time the bell rings, blah-blah-blah. I glanced down the row and saw Natasha sitting up perfectly straight, hanging on every word he said. What a shock, she was a total kiss-up. Ugh.

"Now, let's talk about chair tests."

I faced the podium again, quietly tapping the bell of my horn.

"I expect a lot from each of you," Mr. Dante said. "And I expect each of you to demand a lot from yourselves. We're going to have regular chair tests during class. You'll know ahead of time what I want you to play so you can prepare. After each test, you'll sit according to chair order."

He looked around. "The reason the tests will be frequent is because I want those who put in the extra effort and improve to be rewarded. Each time we have a test, the chair order in your section can potentially change. You might start out sixth chair and be first chair by the end of this semester. It all depends on you."

Interesting. Maybe the new guy wasn't going to be so bad.

"And one more important rule before we warm up." Mr. Dante paused a moment. "It's called no pass, no play. If you fail one of your classes, you won't be eligible to participate in band activities—concerts, football games, contests—until your next progress report or report card is out. We're performing at the football game the Friday after your first six weeks' report card, so make sure you keep up in your classes. Your first progress report is in three weeks, which brings me to the fun part." He smiled again.

"On the last Friday of this month, we'll be having a band party. I'll have more information for you in a few weeks, but for now just remember—you *must* be passing on your progress report to attend."

There were a few murmurs about that, some excited, some nervous. Julia and I grinned at each other. A band party! I went through my closet in my head, the whole no-pass-no-play thing forgotten. I'd never had a problem with my grades.

Mr. Dante started talking about the warm-ups in our folders, but I was daydreaming about the party and Aaron Cook. I wondered if there'd be dancing. Probably not, but the party in my head definitely involved dancing.

I focused when we started to play, though. Maybe I hadn't spent two weeks at Lake Lindon, but I *did* practice all summer, almost every day. (I even made a rehearsal schedule kind of like the one in the Lake Lindon brochure and taped it above my desk. Geeky? For sure. Totally worth it, though.)

As Mr. Dante had us play one at a time to tune, it was easy to tell who hadn't opened their case since May by all the squeaks, wobbly tones, and nervous coughs. Gabby sounded a lot better than the eighth-grader next to her.

I sounded good. Really good.

Brooke sounded okay. So did Owen. I fidgeted in my chair as Natasha lifted her horn.

Ugh. She sounded good, too.

I tapped my fingers softly on the bell of my horn again, waiting as everyone else tuned. Aaron Cook sounded amazing, of course. I remembered at the spring concert last year, he'd had a big solo in one of the songs. And Mrs. Wendell had given him the "Outstanding Seventh-Grade Musician" award. He'd probably been first chair, I realized.

I glanced at Brooke. My chances of being first chair were actually really good. First-chair French horn in the advanced band, as a seventh-grader! Thinking about it made me kind of giddy.

A few chairs down, Natasha coughed lightly. She was looking in her folder, already checking out the music Mr. Dante had given us. I grabbed my own folder and started flipping through the sheets. My eyes widened—tons of notes on the first page, the tempo on the next one was crazy fast, the third was in a time signature I'd never seen before . . .

Whoa. As much as I practiced this summer, maybe it wasn't enough.

Julia and I had lunch right after band. So did Natasha. Apparently, I was doomed to getting zero quality time with my best friend.

We grabbed a table in the corner of the cafeteria and I started pulling stuff out of my bag. (I'd made my lunch the night before—turkey sandwich on wheat bread, cut diagonally; plastic bag with apple slices to avoid the inevitable peel-in-the-teeth scenario that comes with eating it whole; bag of plain potato chips, the least breath-offensive flavor; stick of gum for afterward, just in case. I'd fired Mom from lunch-making duty after the Great Pepperoni Lunchables Catastrophe of last spring.)

"Mr. Dante seems nice," Julia said, breaking off a chunk of cookie. (She was one of those dessert-first people—so weird.) "Maybe a little strict."

I swallowed a bite of sandwich. "Yeah, but I like him. I think the whole frequent-chair-test thing freaked some people out, though."

"I'm going to be dead last in my section." Julia sighed. "I wish Rory or Claire had made advanced band so I wasn't the only seventh-grader. We had so much fun in clarinet class last year." She pulled a banana out of her lunch bag. "You guys are lucky to be in the same section."

Natasha and I smiled at each other uncomfortably. Julia was acting like we were friends already. Because she expected us to be, I realized.

I decided to give it a shot.

"So do you miss your old school?" I asked Natasha, picking at my crust.

She shrugged. "It was okay. I mean, I miss my friends, of course. But they're all on IM, so we still chat a lot. Oh, and we had a *really* good debate team."

She started talking about some debate contest she won and how she'd been captain of the sixth-grade team. I smiled and nodded, bored out of my mind. How could Julia not hear how full of herself her new friend was?

Stop it, I told myself. Julia liked Natasha, and she wanted me to like her, too. I needed to at least give her a chance. Even though she talked about herself a *lot*. And had my backpack. And her nails were professionally manicured and matched her shirt. I stared at her hands, blinking.

This girl was cutting her sandwich with a plastic knife and fork.

She could not be serious.

"So I came in early this morning, and they fixed my schedule." Natasha put down the knife and reached for a bag of M&M's. I had a quick mental image of her daintily cutting each one in half and tried not to laugh.

"Is debate fifth period?" Julia asked.

Natasha shook her head, pulling out her schedule. "No, seventh. I've got math fifth."

"Me too!" Julia squealed, and I grimaced. She glanced at me. "You and I have seventh together, right? Computer lab?"

"Yup."

The three of us spread our schedules on the table (the red and purple map stayed in my bag), and I did a quick assessment. Other than band, Julia and I only had computer lab together. She and Natasha had math and history. Natasha and I were in the same Spanish class during sixth.

Something to look forward to. Stellar.

"Look look look," Natasha hissed suddenly, grabbing Julia's arm and pointing. We all looked up as Seth Anderson passed our table. Julia's face turned bright pink.

"She likes him," Natasha told me with a confidential smile.

I raised my eyebrows at Julia. "Really? We had a few classes with him last year, and she never mentioned it."

Julia rolled her eyes, clearly trying not to smile. "I don't *like* him. He's in our history class, and I told

Natasha he kind of looks like Garrett."

"Who's Garrett?" I was getting annoyed, fast.

Julia and Natasha both sighed, then giggled. I picked up my bag of chips, attempting to arrange my face into an expression that didn't suggest this was the worst lunch period of my life.

"Garrett was this guy at Lake Lindon." Julia watched me struggle to open the stupid bag. "Another clarinet player. We went to the dance together."

"She *kissed* him!" Natasha exclaimed, and the bag exploded in my hands. They both leaned back as chips scattered across the table. I stared at Julia.

"What?"

She ducked her head, grinning and sweeping the crumbs into a pile. "I didn't want to tell you on the phone. But yeah. It happened at the dance." Natasha was doing a little happy dance in her seat. I wanted to puke.

This girl knew about Julia's first kiss before I did.

If there isn't already an actual handbook on best-friendship out there somewhere, there should be. I'd be happy to make it, actually (think of all the potential charts). And I already had a working table of contents in my head. In the chapter called "First Kisses," section one, paragraph one, would say:

Your best friend is the first *person you tell. No exceptions.*

I tried to smile and nod along as Julia told me all the details (*too late*). Then Natasha was off about some other stupid boy at the stupid dance at stupid Lake Lindon, and I tuned out completely.

Staring across the cafeteria, I spotted a familiar smile. Aaron Cook was sitting with a group of guys a few tables away. I didn't really know the rest of them, but some were wearing football jerseys. One of them said something, and Aaron laughed. His eyes kind of squinted when he laughed. And he had creases on both sides of his mouth, like smile parentheses.

For a second, I felt a lot better. Then he glanced up and saw me, and I stared down at my apple slices, horrified. (Horrified and maybe a little excited. I mean, he *looked at me*! That was a good sign, right?)

Natasha and Julia were standing, crumpling up their bags. Apparently I'd missed the bell ringing.

"So you've got science next, right?" Julia asked. She was looking at me funny. I couldn't blame her—I probably looked pretty strange.

"Yeah." I tried to turn so that my back was to Aaron when he left the cafeteria. Julia hugged me.

"We need to catch up," she whispered in my ear. "Seventh period?"

I nodded. "See you then."

I watched her and Natasha walk off to their math class. Then I strapped on the Beacon of Nerdiness and headed the other way. The halls were swarming again. Weird that I felt so alone.

𝄞

The science lab smelled funny. There were several rows of desks in the middle of the room, and small workstations with two stools each lined both walls. I slumped into the nearest desk without looking around and put my head on my arms.

I'd passed apoplectic. Now I really just wanted to go to bed.

When the bell rang, Mrs. Driscoll introduced herself and started the whole first-day spiel all teachers were required to do. I probably should've paid closer attention because this one included lab-safety stuff—what to do in case of broken glass, how to use the fountain in the back in case of burns—but my eyelids were drooping.

Can't. Fall. Asleep. I stared at the huge, brightly colored periodic table of elements on the wall and let my eyes cross so that the colored sections started to move and blur. It kind of looked like *Tetris*.

"Bring your Safety Rules handout and a pencil—everything else can stay at your desk."

My head snapped up. The whole class was moving, heading to the workstations. I grabbed my handout and pencil and stood up. Everyone was pairing up—Mrs. Driscoll must have told us to pick a lab partner. Uh-oh.

Quick survey time. Frantically, I tried to pick out who was left without a partner and spotted Trevor Wells from band. But I'd barely taken a step forward when he pulled up a stool at a workstation with another boy. Before I could really start to freak out, someone tapped me on the shoulder and I spun around.

"Owen!"

"Hey, Holly," Owen said cheerfully. "Do you need a partner?"

"Yes, please." Relieved, I followed him to the last open workstation. Owen and I sat next to each other in beginner French horn class last year. He was really nice (although kind of a dork. But, you know. A nice dork).

I plopped down on the stool and glanced across the room. "Hey, why aren't you and Trevor partners?" They were best friends, at least in sixth grade.

Owen shrugged. "We had a fight at lunch, sort of."

"Oh. Sorry," I said, and he laughed.

"Not a real fight." He flipped over his handout and started doodling on the back, light blond hair hanging in his eyes. "We were playing Warlock, and I used a vorpal blade on his Black Knight."

I stared at him until he looked up. "Owen, I literally have no idea what you just said."

He grinned. "It's a card game, and Trevor's a sore loser. He'll forget about it by tomorrow."

"Ah. Gotcha." I smiled, watching him sketch what looked like a dinosaur on his paper. Probably a dragon, knowing Owen. Yup, now he was adding wings. When Mrs. Driscoll started talking, he flipped it back over and listened.

I tried to listen, too, and failed. So Trevor was over there being a baby about losing some game, but tomorrow he and Owen would be best friends again. Not the same case for me. Tomorrow, right at this moment, Julia would still be sitting in math class with Natasha.

They'd still be sharing secrets that I was apparently not in on, about boys and kisses and who knew what else. The day after that, too, and the rest of the week, and the rest of the year.

I wondered how long it would be before Natasha replaced me completely.

"Holly?"

"Huh?"

Owen was holding a packet of papers out to me, blinking. I realized Mrs. Driscoll was circling the room, handing packets to each workstation.

"Sorry, I just . . . I spaced out." So not like me. I took the packet, embarrassed. "Okay, so . . . so what are we supposed to do?"

"Label the parts of the microscope first." Owen pulled the microscope over so it was sitting between the two of us, then started scribbling on the first page of his own packet. I looked down at mine and saw a drawing of a microscope with a bunch of blank lines.

Trying to look casual, I glanced over my shoulder at the chalkboard. *Eyepiece, condenser, arm, filter holder, illuminator* . . . Apparently while I'd been half asleep, Mrs. Driscoll had gone over this. Not good.

I fidgeted on my stool. I couldn't just look at Owen's paper—I did have *some* pride. But I seriously had no idea what to do.

Think. I stared at the microscope. *Okay, eyepiece. That looks like an eyepiece. Check.* I wrote it on the diagram, then glanced at the board.

Condenser, condenser, condenser, condenser . . .

"Ready for the second page?" Owen was flipping his packet open. Ugh, this was so humiliating.

"No," I admitted. "Sorry, Owen. I wasn't . . . I don't know any of these. I've sort of had a bad day."

"Oh." Owen nodded in understanding. "I thought you looked kind of out of it after lunch. Here, I'll show you." He tapped the top of the microscope with his pencil. "That's the eyepiece."

I laughed. "Yeah, I got that much."

He went through the rest of the diagram, then we moved on to the second page—putting steps for preparing a slide in order. Guess who had no clue what any of the steps were? This girl.

Owen was really nice about it, but I was annoyed with myself. Barely halfway through the first day of seventh grade and I was totally lost in a class and on the verge of losing my best friend.

I had to get it together, and fast.

"He can't be serious with this."

Gabby's breath smelled like Red Hots, even though I was pretty sure she'd left the box in her cubby. She was leaning over, sheet music in her hands, staring at the pages on my music stand. "I mean, really. This is way too hard."

I wanted to say something confident, but in my head I agreed with her. "Labyrinthine Dances" was the craziest piece of music I'd ever seen. The tempo was insanely fast. The time signature changed three times, and the key signature started out okay but then switched to one with a few more flats than I was comfortable with. The first page was only kind of scary, but the second page was *really* ridiculous.

I glanced at Gabby's music, which was positively black with notes. "It's not *that* bad," I said bracingly. Gabby gave me a Look.

"Really? So if this was going to be the chair test

next week instead of the fight song, you'd be okay with that?"

I shrugged, trying to look indifferent, and Gabby rolled her eyes. She was right, of course—I'd been nervous enough ever since Mr. Dante announced our first chair test was coming up. If the test was over *this* music, I'd die.

I took a peek around the room to see what everyone else's reactions were. Julia caught my eye and made a face, and I giggled. The clarinets and flutes were all wearing expressions of varying degrees of disbelief.

To my left, Brooke leaned closer. "What do you think?" she asked quietly. I bit my lip.

"Um . . . yeah, it looks pretty hard," I admitted, and Gabby snickered. To my relief, Brooke nodded in agreement.

"Yeah, we didn't play anything this difficult last year," she said.

I felt better, briefly. Then, on the other side of Owen, I heard Natasha whispering, "I don't know what everyone's freaking out about. We played a piece at *least* this hard at Lake Lindon."

Ugh.

It was Thursday, and over the last four days I'd done everything in my power to like Natasha. But the girl was just stuck-up, plain and simple. She talked about herself constantly. How easy band was. How easy *all* her classes were. How the debate-team coach apparently worshipped the ground she walked on already. She was good at this. She was good at that.

So. Irritating.

I really didn't get why Julia couldn't see it.

"All right." Mr. Dante clapped his hands once, and the mumbling stopped. "Let's talk about this piece a little. Looks pretty challenging, right?"

"It looks *impossible*," said Gabby, and a few of us laughed. Mr. Dante smiled.

"The good news is, we aren't going to be performing this anytime soon," he said. *Well, duh*, I thought. "It's one of the pieces I'd like us to do for contest at the end of this year."

Every spring there was a big contest for middle school bands all over the state. The shelf on the far right side of the band hall was crammed with lots of trophies the Millican advanced band had won from the event. I started tapping my fingers on the bell of my horn, listening.

"We've had almost a week together, and many of you all have already improved a lot. Especially," Mr. Dante added, "those of you who hadn't touched your instruments since last year. I know you might have your doubts, but I believe that by the end of the year, we can perform this successfully. We just need to practice. And that starts"—he leaned over and flipped on the metronome—"right now."

Boop . . . boop . . . boop . . . boop . . .

"Let's try the first eight measures."

Doubtfully, I raised my horn. This tempo was slow.

Like, insanely slow. Mr. Dante counted us off, I drew in a deep breath, and we played.

Four measures in and I was ready to fall out of my chair. I thought playing fast was hard—playing slow was *killing* me. Behind me, I heard a few of the tuba players give up mid-note to suck in a breath. I struggled not to rush and accidentally played an A-flat instead of an A.

It took us an hour to play the eight measures. Okay, it *felt* like an hour. Imagine strapping heavy bricks to your feet and trying to walk through knee-deep mud. That's what playing this song was like. Hard, tedious, and pointless.

Mr. Dante flipped the metronome off. "I'd like everyone to have a look at the first sixteen measures by Monday," he said. "We'll be working on this one regularly, each time just a little bit faster. By spring, it'll be a piece of cake."

I gave Gabby a sidelong glance. She looked back, eyes wide. "He can't—"

"Yeah," I interrupted her. "I think he's serious."

The first day of science had been maybe a little intimidating. But by Friday, it was more like terrifying.

I had no idea what was going on.

I mean *none*. I wasn't, like, a perfect student or anything, but my grades had always been pretty good. But now I felt like science could actually be my first C.

Or worse. My stomach tensed at the thought as I tried to decipher this week's lab assignment. The band party was in three weeks, right after our first progress reports came out. And if I actually managed to fail science, I wouldn't be going.

Resolutely, I sat up straight on my stool and set down the packet Mrs. Driscoll had given us at the start of class. Owen was already setting up the microscope. Next to it was a plate with a small piece of onion skin and a few toothpicks.

"Ready?" he asked.

"Yes."

"Okay, first we'll do the onion."

Nodding, I took the little glass slide and placed the piece of onion on it.

"Hang on." Owen pushed a small dropper toward me. "We have to put water on the slide first."

"Oh." *Dang it.* I picked up the onion piece and squeezed a little drop of water on the slide. "There. Um . . . oh, now we put it here, right?" I started to transfer the slide over to the microscope.

"Wait!" Grabbing another bottle, Owen took the slide and dropped more liquid on top of the onion. "Iodine," he explained. "See, it's in step four."

I looked down at my packet. Yup, step four—iodine. I grimaced.

It had been like this all week. Mrs. Driscoll would say a bunch of stuff I didn't really understand, I'd try to read my textbook but it was like Greek or something, and then we'd head to our workstations for a lab and I'd be totally lost. We got a daily grade for lab assignments, and as much as I hated to admit it, I'd have failed them all if it wasn't for Owen.

"Are you okay?" He looked kind of worried.

"Yeah. Stellar." I blew a strand of brown hair out of my eyes. "Sorry I'm such a sucky lab partner."

Owen blinked. "You're not!"

"Liar." I grinned at him. Honestly, I was really grateful Owen hadn't ditched me. On Tuesday, just like he said, he and Trevor had been friends again. Trevor had even asked me before class started if we could switch lab partners. (No wonder—his partner, Brent McEwan, picked his nose like there was money up there or something. Not someone I'd want to share a microscope with.)

Luckily, Owen refused to switch before I could even answer Trevor. "Maybe now he won't be such a baby about losing," Owen had said, laughing when Trevor stormed off back to his workstation.

I watched him put the onion slide into place, and we took turns examining it. I drew what I saw—blobs with dots in them—on my packet. Then we used the toothpicks to scrape the insides of our cheeks, smeared that on a slide (ew), and examined it. Oh, hey, more blobs and dots. I drew them, then read the next question.

What did the onion cell contain that the cheek cell did not?

Um, they were both a bunch of blobs and dots. And somehow I didn't think "blob" or "dot" would be an acceptable answer, anyway. My fingers drummed nervously on the table as I waited for Owen to finish.

Mrs. Driscoll started writing weekend reminders on the board. I squinted to read the last one. *Quiz on animal and vegetable cells next Wednesday.* My stomach clenched up again.

I had to study this weekend, or I was going to be in serious trouble.

"Unlike animal cells, plant cells are surrounded by a protective cell wall, which is made up of cellulose. Plant cells also have organelles, such as chloroplast and . . ." I stopped, squeezing my eyes shut. "Wait, what's an organelle?"

I flipped to the glossary in the back of my textbook and read aloud. "'*Organelle*: a specialized part of a cell with a specific function.' Oh, I totally get it now. Thanks."

It was Saturday afternoon, and I was lying on my bed talking to my science book. Clearly, my weekend had been stellar so far.

Flipping back to the first chapter, I started reading the same paragraph. For the third time. It was still pretty much meaningless.

The phone rang, and I tossed my book in the air. "*I got it!*" I hollered, lunging for the phone on my night table. "Hello?"

"It's me!"

At the sound of Julia's voice, I smiled for what felt like the first time in a month. "Hey! What's up?"

"Want to go to the movies? My dad offered to drive."

"Yes yes yes yes *yes*." I was already on my feet and heading to the closet. "I'm dying to see *House of the Wicked*, I saw this one scene online and—"

"Nooo!" Julia wailed, and I grinned. "No horror movies, I'm begging you. Besides, Natasha wants to see *Seven Dates*."

I froze, a pink-striped sleeve clenched in my hand. "What?"

"I know it's not your thing," she went on quickly. "But it looks really cute, and I kind of want to see it, too. You might like it if you give it a shot! Even though there's no possessed people or creepy girls crawling out of holes in the ground."

"Um . . . hang on a sec," I said, then pressed my hand over the mouthpiece. I stared at the pink shirt, still dangling crookedly off the hanger.

Natasha was going. I should have known.

I had a tendency to overthink stuff a little bit. According to Mom, anyway. But I couldn't help it. And in about three seconds, this was what went through my brain:

1. Had Natasha called Julia and asked her to see a movie, and then Julia called to see if I wanted to come?

2. Probably not, because Julia said her dad was going to drive them. So seeing a movie had been Julia's idea.

3. But when she called, she already knew what movie Natasha wanted to see. Therefore:

4. Julia invited Natasha to go before she invited me.

I swallowed hard, then pressed the phone to my ear.

"Hey, I'm back. Um . . . my mom says I can't go. I forgot we, um . . . we're all supposed to go out to dinner tonight. You know. Family thing."

"Oh." Julia sounded disappointed. I wondered if she knew I was lying. "Yeah, okay. Maybe next weekend."

"Sure, yeah. Have fun!"

"Thanks. I'll call you tomorrow, okay?"

"All right."

I flopped back on my bed and stared at the ceiling for a few seconds. Okay, like half an hour. I was almost asleep when Chad slammed the door downstairs, jolting me awake. (I knew it was Chad because everyone else in the house knew how to close a door without the whole neighborhood hearing it.)

I had to do something. I had to do something that was *not* studying science. Imagining Julia and Natasha hanging out was driving me nuts. Watching some sappy romance movie, to make matters worse.

"Gee, I wonder what happens," I said, standing up. "I bet there's a guy who likes a girl, even though she's boring as dirt. And she likes him back, even though he's boring as dirt, too. But there's some big misunderstanding that keeps them apart."

I kicked my science book, sending it skidding over

to my bedroom door. "So one of them probably ends up dating some jerk, even though everyone in the movie knows they're a jerk. But by the end they figure it out and the guy and girl end up together, just like every single person in the audience knew they would."

Talking to myself was not helping me feel better. My gaze fell on my horn case. Chair test this week. Without wasting another second, I pulled out my horn and music and sat at my desk.

Twenty minutes later, I'd played the part Mr. Dante chose for the horn test ten times in a row perfectly. (It was pretty easy, honestly—I was surprised he hadn't picked a harder test.) Natasha was going down. Just thinking about getting first chair and seeing the look on her face made me smile. I lifted up my horn and started again, but only got about three measures in before my door flew open.

"Chad!" I yelled. "You're supposed to knock."

He fell down on his knees and put his hands together like he was praying. "Please, Holly. I'm begging you. I can't watch a movie when it sounds like there's a constipated moose in the room next door."

I rolled my eyes. "Deal with it. I have to practice."

"All day?" he whined.

"Seriously, Chad, it hasn't even been half an hour." Holding my horn over the trash can, I pressed a valve and water dripped onto a few crumpled tissues.

Chad stared. "What are you doing?"

"Emptying my spit valve."

He made an exaggeratedly grossed-out face. "That's your *spit*? Nasty!"

It was unbelievable that this guy was almost four years older than me.

"Chad, get out. I have a chair test this week."

He started to whine again but got cut off by a hand smacking the back of his head. "Ow!"

"Leave your sister alone." Mom pushed past him and stepped into my room. "She needs to practice."

"But I'm trying to watch a—"

"Use your headphones." Turning her back on Chad, Mom held out a shopping bag. "Sorry I couldn't get to the store this week! Work's been crazy. They didn't have the light blue, but I thought this one was cute."

I reached into the bag and pulled out a turquoise backpack with purple pockets. Quickly, I scanned through my closet in my mind—I had six outfits that would go with this. No, seven. "Thanks, Mom!"

"Anytime." She backed up and nearly tripped over Chad, who was still kneeling on the floor like a moron. "Would you get up already?" Mom cried, ruffling his hair. Then she spotted my science book. "Holly, what's that doing on the floor?"

"Oh—whoops." I picked it up hastily.

"Oh my God, you were studying, weren't you. On a Saturday." Chad shook his head, heaving himself to his feet.

"Something you should try sometime," Mom chided him. She glanced at me. "Are classes going okay, honey?"

I smiled tightly. "Yeah. Of course."

"Of course." She smiled back. "Pizza tonight. I'll call Spins at around six for delivery—meaning, please don't eat an entire bag of Cheetos at five thirty," she added, giving Chad a Look before slipping past him and heading downstairs.

Chad started to leave, but I stopped him. "Hey, what movie are you watching?"

"*Watch the Fog*. The second one."

"Ooh, that is a good one." (Besides our blue eyes, awesome taste in movies was the only thing my brother and I had in common.) "Hey, want to go see *House of the Wicked*?"

Chad squinted. He did this pretty much every time he had to think, which wasn't too often. Like he needed to physically squeeze his brain into action. "Can you get into that one?"

"Yup, it's PG-13. Maybe tomorrow?"

"I've got plans at three. We could do an earlier show if you want. *Not* before noon," he added. "You know I need my beauty sleep."

"Chad, all you do is sleep." I smiled sweetly at him. "I don't think it's working."

He made a face. "Have fun blowing spit all over the place," he said, then shut the door before I could retort.

Well, at least the weekend wouldn't be a total bust. Seeing a good movie with my loser brother was better than seeing stupid *Seven Dates* with a girl who probably got all weepy at the mind-numbingly happy ending.

I glared at my music for a minute, then realized my fingers were drumming rather loudly on the bell. Gritting my teeth, I grabbed my horn and took a deep breath. Time to practice.

Chapter Seven

"Come on, Julia. Where are you?"

I glanced at my watch, then at the clock on the wall. (Still synced.) Ninety seconds before the first bell, and Julia still wasn't here. I started fiddling with my necklace—a silver chain with a little turtle made of colored glass. Julia got it for me at the beach. She had a matching one, except hers was a starfish.

It was Wednesday. Julia had been acting kind of weird all week. She'd probably picked up on the fact that I didn't like Natasha. I couldn't help it—I tried. But I was stressed out enough without having to deal with Natasha the Perfect.

This afternoon was the dreaded science quiz, and apparently I was more than a little anxious, because my stomach was doing this squirmy thing. Aaron Cook did not help matters one bit when he walked down the hall looking far cuter than any boy had the right to.

I stared at the floor, watching him from the corner

of my eye. Here I was, standing alone at a locker that wasn't even mine. And now he was slowing down. He was slowing down. He was *stopping right next to me.*

I forced myself to look up. Aaron was spinning the lock on the locker two away from Julia's. How? How had I been in school a week and a half and only just now was learning that my best friend's locker was right next to Aaron Cook's?

Briefly, I considered opening Julia's locker and burying my head in it. I knew her combination.

Don't be a chicken. I stood there dumbly, still twisting the little glass turtle. *Just say something.* He was alone, which was pretty unusual. The perfect opportunity.

Okay, here I go. I took a deep breath. *No, I can't do it. Yes, I can. No, I can't. Yes, I—*

"Hey, Holly."

Oh my God.

I glanced up and tried to look like I hadn't been extremely aware of his presence for the past minute. "Hey, Aaron. What's up?" Not bad. Okay. I could do this.

"Not much." Aaron stuffed a book into his bag and smiled at me. "Cool necklace."

Oh. My. God.

"Thanks!" My voice sounded weirdly high. Probably because I'd stopped breathing entirely. "I . . . um . . ."

"Aaron!" I was saved by the tallest eighth-grader I'd ever seen in my life. He was like a red-haired giant. "Coach wants to see you before lunch."

"About what?" Aaron shut his locker. The giant shrugged.

"Practice after school, I think. We're supposed to bring . . ."

I didn't hear the rest of the conversation because they were walking away and I was still standing at Julia's locker turning purple from oxygen deprivation. *Breathe, dummy.*

I inhaled, exhaled, and laughed. Aaron Cook had talked to me. Again. And I talked back. And he *liked my necklace.* I resisted the urge to kiss the little glass turtle. I had to tell Julia about this immediately.

But when the bell rang a minute later, I was still standing at her locker alone, because she'd never shown up. My smile faded, and I picked up my bag and headed down the hall. No sign of Natasha, either, and they had history together first period.

I wondered if Julia was avoiding me.

Something was definitely up. Julia seemed okay during band, but at lunch I could tell there was something she wasn't telling me. When something bothered Julia, she would pick her food apart with her fingers before she ate it, and her laugh would change. It'd turn into this forced, high-pitched noise.

Five minutes into lunch and she'd broken a chocolate bar into about a dozen pieces and giggled at three things Natasha said (none of which were funny).

Like I said, something was definitely up.

Then again, I wasn't exactly feeling normal, either. I'd never really had to worry about a class before. I'd spent Monday and Tuesday night trying to read my science textbook, and I was pretty much ready to set it on fire. I'd been skating by on the labs thanks to Owen, but I had to face facts. It wasn't just that I might not ace the quiz; I was totally lost in that class.

By the time I got to science, my stomach was churning so much that I probably could've gotten away with just going to the nurse's office.

"Hi, Holly!"

"Hey, Owen." I slid into the desk next to his and tossed my backpack down. He glanced at it and made a weird face. "What?" I asked.

"Nothing," Owen said. "Just, um . . . what happened to the Batman bag you had last week, anyway?"

I snorted. "I was only using that because my brother ruined my real backpack. This one's new."

"Oh." He looked disappointed, for some reason.

"Sorry," I said teasingly. "Didn't realize you were such a big Batman fan."

Owen blinked rapidly. He did that a lot when he was confused, I'd learned. "I'm not, actually. Just thought it was kind of cool that you were."

Huh. Apparently Owen and I had pretty different definitions of "cool."

While Mrs. Driscoll took roll, I flipped through the chapter on cells in a desperate last-minute attempt to learn . . . well, anything. Then she was handing out the quizzes. I held my breath as she placed one on my desk. Multiple choice! Score. Maybe this wouldn't be so bad.

1. A mitochondrion is a type of:

A) cell

B) lipid

C) organelle

D) chloroplast

Oh no.

My heart started pounding as I scanned the rest of the questions. This had never, ever happened to me before. I had no idea what to do. Panicked, I gripped my pen and glanced furtively around the room.

Next to me, Owen's pencil was scratching away. Every time he read another question, he tapped the eraser against his mouth.

When he did it again, his hand moved up and I could see his paper.

I looked back at my own quiz quickly. No, I couldn't do that. I couldn't cheat—I'd *never* cheated.

But I didn't know what else to do.

Mrs. Driscoll was walking slowly up and down the aisles. I waited until she passed me, then glanced at Owen again. His pencil was moving, then it stopped . . .

Suddenly, even though he didn't look right at me, I knew he knew what I was doing. He hesitated, his hand hovering over his paper. Trying to decide whether or not to let me copy. He was probably two seconds away from blinking his eyelids right off.

I looked back at my own paper quickly. I couldn't use Owen like that. Guilty tears burned in my eyes, and I set my pencil down to rub them away.

Twenty minutes later Mrs. Driscoll collected our quizzes and I felt like I had a rock in my stomach. There was no way I'd passed, and I couldn't even look at Owen. When class ended, I hurried up to Mrs. Driscoll's desk as everyone else filed out.

"Mrs. Driscoll, can you please grade my quiz now?" I asked in a rush.

She smiled. "Worried, Holly? You shouldn't be—I hear you're an excellent student."

"I am—I mean, thanks," I said, blushing. "But I . . . this chapter was kind of confusing."

"Well, let's see how you did." Mrs. Driscoll found my quiz and picked up her red pen. I watched as she read, then marked an X. Then another. Then another. After the sixth one, she looked up at me, her smile gone.

"I failed, didn't I?" My eyes were burning again. Mrs. Driscoll nodded sympathetically.

"But, Holly, this is only the first quiz," she added. "Your lab grades have been fine so far! You can still bring up your grade."

"In time for the first progress report, though? Because if I'm failing this class on my progress report I can't go to the band party or play at the pep rally, and if

I fail on the report card I can't play at the football game and—"

"Holly!" Mrs. Driscoll held her hand up. "Listen, you're going to be fine. We're having a test in less than two weeks. So long as you pass that, you'll have a passing grade on your progress report. My tutoring hours are Tuesdays and Thursdays before school." She patted my hand in what I guessed was supposed to be a reassuring way. "Don't worry, it'll be okay."

"Okay."

But by the time I got to sixth period, I felt anything but fine. One test in science was going to determine whether or not I could go to the band party. And I had less than two weeks to figure out how to pass it.

"It was so easy. I mean, like, kindergarten easy." Natasha stabbed a piece of sandwich with her fork. "I can't believe I was so worried about being in advanced math."

I wanted to puke. And it had nothing to do with my lunch.

But I just smiled and peeled my orange. "That's awesome, Natasha! I know what you mean—I was kind of nervous about that Spanish essay yesterday. But I ended up getting a ninety-eight!" I chewed on an orange slice, enjoying the way her face tightened.

"Oh. Good for you, that's great."

(I didn't normally brag like Natasha. But we were in the same Spanish class and yesterday Mr. Hernandez had asked me to pass everyone's essays out, so I knew Natasha only got a ninety-two. And she *knew* I knew. Take that, Miss Perfect.)

"Did you guys watch *Save Me* last night? New

episode," Julia said abruptly. I glanced down; there was a pile of cracker crumbs on her napkin, and she was in the process of destroying another one. I felt a pang of guilt.

"Yeah, I did. Can you believe they—"

"Julia!" Natasha interrupted with a squeal. "There's Seth!"

We all turned to look as Seth Anderson joined the lunch line. He *was* pretty cute, I had to admit. I tried not to think about Garrett of First Kiss Fame and smiled at Julia.

"You've got PE with him, right?"

Her face was pink. "Yeah. He's in the orchestra, too. Cello."

"Too bad he's not in band," Natasha said. "Then you'd see him at the party. Hey, do you know what you're wearing yet? That sort of flowery dress you wore to the dance at band camp would be perfect!"

And we were back on Lake Lindon. *Again.* I forced myself not to scowl—Natasha always did this on purpose, and I refused to let her know it got to me. She and Julia started talking about who wore what at the oh-so-epic dance that I didn't get to go to. Sighing, I surveyed the cafeteria. Staring at Aaron Cook would keep me entertained.

But I saw Owen first. He hadn't acted weird during band, but with Brooke between us, it wasn't like we got to talk a lot. Every time I thought about what I'd almost done in science, the knot in my stomach would tighten. I glanced at Natasha, who was now describing the outfit she was wearing to the band party in way too much detail.

"Be right back, guys." I got up quickly and headed over to Owen before I could change my mind.

"Hi, Owen."

He looked surprised when I slid into the seat next to him. On his other side, Trevor was arguing with a few boys I didn't know. A pile of cards with elves and swords and stuff on them were spread out in the middle of the table. I grinned.

"He's losing again, huh?"

Owen laughed. "Like always." He was doodling something on the back of a napkin. It looked like some sort of troll.

"So, Owen, um . . ." I paused, unsure of what I even wanted to say. "Promise you won't tell anyone this."

"Um, okay . . ."

I lowered my voice.

"I kind of massively failed that science quiz yesterday."

Owen blinked. "What? How do you know?"

"I asked Mrs. Driscoll to grade it after class." I swallowed. "Come on, Owen—you know I have no idea what's going on in there."

"Well . . ." He glanced at me. "I guess I didn't know you were having that much trouble with it."

"If I don't pass the test we're having the week after next, I'll fail on my progress report. And you know Mr. Dante's rule about band."

His gray eyes widened in understanding. "Oh. Okay." Owen paused, tapping his pencil on the troll drawing. "Well, if you want, I can help you."

I let out a breath. "I was hoping you'd say that. But seriously—I'm really, *really* lost."

Owen shrugged. "It's only been a week and a half. You can catch up." He glanced at the pile of cards, brow furrowed. "Actually . . . I have an idea. Can you come over Friday after school?"

"Yes. Definitely." I leaned back in my chair, relieved. "Thanks, Owen."

"You're welcome."

"And hey, how do you know my brother?"

"Huh?"

I tapped the troll on the napkin. "Dead ringer, seriously."

Owen laughed, and the knot in my stomach finally started to loosen.

𝄞

My science-quiz nerves were nothing compared to how I felt before band on Friday. The chair test was a totally different thing—unlike science, I actually knew what I was doing in band. I could play the test from memory, and I sounded good.

But this wasn't about sounding good. It was about sounding better than everyone else. And by everyone, I meant Natasha.

I grabbed my horn and music folder and started heading out of the cubby room. Julia was already in her chair with her reed in her mouth, and Natasha was kneeling next to her. They were giggling about something. I turned abruptly and headed back to my cubby.

On the surface, everything was fine between Julia and me. We had computer lab together last period, and we talked and joked around like nothing was weird. But she was still picking her food apart at lunch, and she still looked sad sometimes when she thought I wasn't looking. Whatever was bothering her, she didn't want to talk about it with me.

Which meant *I* was the thing that was bothering her.

"Hey, Holly?" Gabby was standing by the trash can, a box of Red Hots in her hand. "Did you write down the essay assignment for English tomorrow? I spaced out."

"Yeah. 'Compare and contrast your favorite season with your least favorite.' No, thanks," I added when she offered the box.

"Cool, thanks." Polishing off the candy, Gabby tossed the box into the trash and knelt down at her cubby. As she hung the strap around her neck, I peered curiously inside her case.

"Why is your reed already on your mouthpiece?" I asked. "I thought you guys were supposed to take everything apart every day, like the clarinets do. And, like, clean it and stuff."

Gabby shrugged. "Yeah, we are. But it's faster this way."

"Ew!" I exclaimed. "Didn't Mrs. Wendell tell your class about what could happen if you don't clean your instrument every day?"

Grinning, Gabby slid her case back into her cubby. "I guess I forgot. What happens, Mrs. Mead?"

I decided to ignore that. "Gunk builds up inside and could even start growing mold. *Mold*, Gabby."

Gabby clapped her hand to her cheek. "Oh, the horror!"

I stared at her in disbelief. "Why are you laughing? Are you seriously not grossed out about putting a moldy mouthpiece in your mouth?"

But she was still laughing as we headed to our seats.

A few of the trumpet players were playing through the chair test. Suddenly, a fresh wave of nervousness hit me. I'd been so focused on beating Natasha that I kind of forgot we had to play the test in front of everyone.

Mr. Dante started the chair test right after our warm-ups, thank God. I'd have died if he'd waited till the end of rehearsal.

Leaning back in my chair, I closed my eyes as the flutes played one at a time, then the clarinets. It took a massive effort to keep my fingers still. When Julia's turn came, I opened my eyes.

She did pretty well, but I could tell she was nervous. The whole clarinet section *was* pretty amazing, though.

The saxophones were up next. There was only one bari sax and one tenor sax player, but Mr. Dante made them do the chair test anyway. Then there were three alto saxes—two eighth-graders and Gabby. She gave me a little grin right before her turn.

"Wish me luck," she whispered.

It took about three seconds of her playing for me to forget about her gross no-cleaning policy. Gabby was *awesome*. I knew the music for this test was pretty easy, but she made it sound so . . . effortless.

I was so wowed that I almost forgot about my turn.

"Holly?" Mr. Dante prompted me.

Blinking, I sat up straight and adjusted my music stand. I tried to pretend I was back in my room, but honestly, it was impossible not to be aware of the forty-something kids sitting all around me in dead silence.

I gave myself a split-second mental pep talk. *You did not spend all those hours practicing just to get freaked out because people can hear you. People are* supposed to *hear you. That's why you're in band.*

Then I played.

It was over in about twenty seconds. And I totally nailed it.

I sat back in my chair, trying not to look smug. But seriously—I'd played it perfectly.

"Nice job," Gabby murmured, and I grinned.

"You too."

I kept my eyes fixed on my horn while Brooke played, trying to keep the smile off my face. She sounded fine, but she flubbed one tiny part. Owen sounded a lot better than he did last year, but he messed up a measure and had to play it again.

Time for Natasha to play. I held my breath as she lifted her horn.

She was good.

Okay, she was really, really good.

Still, by the time she finished, I wasn't convinced she was better than me. Leaning back in my chair again, I bit my lip. Natasha hadn't made any big mistakes, but she'd sounded . . . different than I had. And I'd played exactly what was on the page.

So I must have sounded better. Mr. Dante had to have noticed. I relaxed a little bit. By the end of rehearsal, I was feeling good about my chances at first chair again.

After I put my instrument away, I hurried over to Julia's cubby. "Well, that wasn't too bad."

Julia made a face. "I was awful. Last chair, here I come."

"No you weren't!" I meant it—maybe Julia wouldn't be first chair, but she'd sounded fine. "Anyway, everyone in your section is really good. And we'll have another chair test in a few weeks, so things could change."

She shrugged. "Yeah, I guess. You sounded great, though!"

I beamed. "Thanks!"

Julia placed her reed in its little case, then wiped her mouthpiece before putting it away. (I should ask her to give Gabby cleaning lessons.) "Yeah, you and

Natasha were best in your section for sure."

Suddenly, smiling was a little harder to do.

"Hey, I almost forgot!" Julia straightened up, pulling her backpack on. "Want to come over after school today? Dad's making fajitas."

"Awesome!" Julia's dad was an amazing cook. "What time? I can . . ." I trailed off when I noticed Owen chatting with Trevor by his cubby. We were supposed to study today. I'd totally forgotten.

"Um, I . . . I can't," I said lamely. "I have to—"

"Look at this!" Natasha appeared out of nowhere next to Julia, flapping her hand around. "I just chipped my nail on my case."

Julia examined her finger. "It's not that bad. Can you bring some polish tonight? We'll fix it."

"Definitely." Natasha gave me her best fake smile. "You're coming too, right, Holly? Fajita night?"

"I asked her during first period," Julia told me hastily. "So you can't come, really? Why not?"

Great. I so wasn't about to tell Natasha that I was getting tutored in science. "I'm, um . . . my uncle's in town. We're going out to dinner."

I hated lying to Julia. Like, really, really, *really* hated. And I knew she could tell I was lying.

"It's okay," she said as the bell rang. "Maybe next time."

We squeezed out of the band hall into the already crowded halls. "See you seventh period!" I tried to sound normal.

Julia waved. "See you!" She was trying to sound normal, too. Neither of us did, though.

I joined the horde of bodies moving toward the math hall and wondered if our friendship would ever really be back to normal.

Chapter Nine

By the time Owen and I got to his house, I was feeling pretty rotten. When Owen opened his front door, we were immediately attacked by a fuzzy black-and-tan blob. It turned out being sad was pretty much impossible with a puppy licking my face.

"His name's Worf," Owen said as I plopped down on the floor. Worf leaped into my lap and I started scratching his belly, giggling when he squirmed and made these little whimpering noises.

"How old is he?"

"Just a few months." Owen picked up a rubber bone and squeaked it. We laughed as Worf ran in circles, barking frantically. "We got him over summer break."

"Owen, is that you?"

"Hi, Mom!" Owen tossed the bone down the hallway, and Worf took off after it. "This is Holly."

Owen's mom had the same light blond hair as him, except it looked like she actually combed hers. They had the same smile, too. "Ah, the lab partner. Nice to meet you, Holly."

I scrambled to my feet. "Hi, Mrs. Reynolds. Nice to meet you."

"It's Mrs. Grady, actually," she said kindly, glancing around. "No Trevor today?"

"I told him to come over later," Owen said, picking up his bag. I grabbed mine, too, relieved that Trevor wouldn't be studying with us. The fewer people that knew I was actually failing a class, the better.

"Is Steve still at work?" Owen asked.

Mrs. Grady nodded. "He'll be home in a few hours. Have fun, you two!"

I followed Owen upstairs. "Who's Steve?"

"My stepdad," he replied. "So this is the game room," he added when we reached the top of the stairs. I looked around. *No kidding.*

One long sofa sat in the middle of the room facing an enormous TV, with at least three different game consoles and, like, twenty controllers on the floor in front of it. Next to the TV were stacks of shoe boxes stuffed with discs and cartridges. The computer desk along the right wall was cluttered with even more games. I couldn't even see the surface of the coffee table because it was covered in those cards he was always playing with at lunch. Posters of robots and dragons and spaceships were tacked up all over the walls, and I had to shove aside a dozen comic books just to sit on the sofa.

This place was like Nerd Central.

I got out my science textbook while Owen cleared the coffee table. Carefully, he divided the cards up into two stacks. Then he held one stack out to me.

"Um, Owen?" I said, eyeing the cards. "I thought you were going to help me with science."

"I am!" He set the cards down on my book. I picked up the top one and examined it. These weren't the same cards from lunch, although at first glance, they could've been. The first one had a picture that kind of looked like one of the cell illustrations in our textbook, except it was floating in what I was pretty sure was supposed to be a witch's cauldron. I flipped the card over.

CENTRIOLE
Pair of organelles found in animal cells

There was a whole bunch of other stuff written on it, none of which I understood. I looked at Owen uncertainly.

"Okay, say you play that card first." He took it from me and placed it on the table. "My turn." He held up a card with a picture of a long, curved blade chopping an onion. I raised my eyebrows.

"Remember the onion skin lab we did?" Owen asked.

"Yeah . . ."

"So is an onion a plant or an animal?" I glared at

him without answering, and he laughed. "Okay, so I have a plant cell, and you have a centriole. Are there centrioles in plant cells?"

Okay . . . Owen was nice, but maybe he was kind of insane, too. I looked at my centriole card again. "It says it's in animal cells. So . . . no?"

"Right!" He slid his onion card next to my card. "So you win that hand. But if I'd picked this one"—he waved a card with a mouse wearing a wizard's hat on it—"then I would've won. Get it?"

"Sort of." I narrowed my eyes. "So hang on—you let me win?"

Owen shrugged. "Just this hand, to show you how—"

"Don't do that anymore." I sat up straight, shuffling through my cards. "Okay, let's play."

Ten minutes later, this game was actually starting to make sense. After a while, I was kind of rocking it.

"Ha." I slapped down a card with a leaf triumphantly. "I'll take that chloroplast card, thank you very much. What?" Owen looked like he was trying not to laugh.

"Nothing." He grinned. "Just . . . I bet you really hate losing, don't you?"

I rolled my eyes. "Does anyone *like* it? Who wants to be a loser?"

"Like it or not, everyone's a loser at some point." Owen tossed his cards down, glancing at the clock. "Want to take a break? We could play a video game."

I was startled to realize we'd been playing for way

over an hour. Mr. Gordon was probably heating up the grill for fajitas right now, while Julia and Natasha painted each other's nails. I pushed that image out of my mind.

"Yeah, sure."

"Which one?" Owen asked, kneeling down next to the stacks of shoe boxes.

"Doesn't matter."

He glanced at me, but didn't say anything. I picked up one of the cards and examined it while Owen put in a game and plugged in the controllers.

"Owen, did you make these?"

"Yeah."

"Why? And what's with all the dragons and swords and stuff?"

He turned on the TV and plopped back down next to me. "Last year I had Mr. Adams for history—did you?" I shook my head. "His class was really hard. I failed two tests in a row because I couldn't keep all the dates and names straight. My mom kept saying it was ridiculous that I couldn't remember who was president during World War I, but I have all seventeen of the forbidden spells memorized. From Warlock," Owen explained, handing me a controller. "So I made a card game for history, kind of based off that game. I think part of the reason I can remember all that stuff in Warlock is the pictures. I thought it might help you, too."

I stared at the cards. "Owen, that is really . . . cool."

He turned a little red. "Yeah, right."

"No, it really is!" I meant it, too. Sure, making an elaborate card game to study ranked Owen pretty high on the dork-o-meter. But hey—I finally knew what an organelle was. "Thanks for doing this."

"You're welcome."

I glanced at the TV. "*Prophet Wars*. So . . . is this more warlocks?"

"Nope." Owen picked up his controller. "Aliens."

"Nice."

It didn't take long to realize I was a spectacular failure at this game. In five minutes I'd gotten blown to bits, like, eight times. I ground my teeth, thumbs flying over my controller.

Make that nine.

"Wow, you're really bad at this."

I glanced up in surprise and crashed my tank into the side of a building. A bunch of aliens crawled out and dragged me away from the wreckage. Trevor flopped down on the sofa between me and Owen, and I glared at him.

"That one was your fault."

He snorted. "Yeah, because you were doing so awesome before."

"Shut up, Trevor." Owen got up and grabbed a third controller, but I handed Trevor mine.

"It's okay, I've got to go. My mom said she'd be here at five." I definitely was not in the mood to get my butt kicked again, and especially not by Trevor. "Thanks, Owen."

"Sure." He followed me downstairs. "So we just studied the first chapter today, but I think the test will cover three."

"Right." I smiled as Worf came bounding out of the kitchen. "Um, so . . . can I come over again next week? To study?"

"Yeah! I'll make more cards."

I knelt down to scratch Worf one more time. "I can't believe I'm so nervous about this stupid test. I'm actually more worried about it than I was about the chair test in band."

Owen looked surprised. "Were you nervous today? I couldn't tell."

"Really?" I laughed. "I was. I was *really* nervous."

"Well, you sounded great." Owen grabbed a piece of rope and started a tug-of-war with Worf.

"Thanks!" I hesitated, watching him. "I . . . I really want first chair."

He dangled the rope in the air, and Worf danced around on his hind legs. "I bet you get it."

I smiled, fiddling with the straps of my backpack. "You don't think . . . you don't think Natasha will get it?" I asked, trying to keep my voice as casual as possible.

Owen just shrugged. "Well, maybe. She's really good, too."

Ugh.

I stayed quiet a little bit too long, and he gave me a curious look. "I mean, you're both good. It doesn't really matter who's first and who's second, does it?"

I smiled tightly. "Nah, I guess not." Shouldering my backpack, I opened the front door. "See you Monday, Owen."

"See you."

On the ride home, Mom turned on the radio. But in my head I heard myself play the chair test, and then Natasha, over and over. I'd sounded better. I *had*. I wondered if she was obsessing over it, too. I wondered if she was asking Julia who sounded better right now over fajitas.

Everyone's a loser at some point. I stared at the window and made a face at my reflection.

Maybe everyone had to lose every once in a while. But when it came to band and best friends, I was so not losing to Natasha.

On Monday, I got to school early and went straight to the band hall. No chair test results yet. I spent the next three class periods quietly stressing to death. When Gabby shook her box of Red Hots under my nose, I almost puked in my cubby.

"You okay?" she asked, and I nodded. "You look kind of—oh, hey, check it out!"

Gabby pointed, and I looked out into the band hall. Mr. Dante was taping a piece of paper to his office door; five or six kids were already crowded around.

"Sit in chair order today," I heard him say, and my heart pretty much stopped.

"Cool, let's go look!" Gabby hurried out of the cubby room, still hooking her sax to her neck strap. It was hard not to sprint across the room, but somehow I managed. Holding my breath, I reached the door and found my section on the list.

French Horn

1. *Natasha Prynne*
2. *Holly Mead*
3. *Brooke Dennis*
4. *Owen Reynolds*

This could not be right.

I stared at the results, a wave of numbness washing over me. Turning, I dodged elbows and horns as more kids crowded around the door and walked slowly to my seat.

Second chair. Second best.

Gabby plopped down in her regular seat. "Congrats!" she said cheerfully, and I looked at her blankly. Was she joking?

"Huh?"

She raised an eyebrow. "Um, congrats?" she repeated. "Second chair, that's really good."

Oh my God, she was serious. I forced myself to smile. "Oh, thanks. Congrats to you, too."

"Thanks!" Gabby was first chair alto sax—no surprise there. I looked down at my horn, very aware of the empty seat between us and the girl who was about to sit in it.

"Take your seats, please!" Mr. Dante called. I closed my eyes as everyone found their chairs. It was bad enough that I'd cried in science—I was *not* doing it in band. Especially with Natasha right next to me.

I couldn't ignore her, though. Taking a deep breath, I looked up just as she sat next to me.

"Hey." My voice sounded normal—cheerful, even. Good.

"Hey." Natasha fake-smiled, and I fake-smiled right back.

Yeah, this was going to be stellar.

Rehearsal seemed to drag on forever. When Mr. Dante finally told us to pack up, I was relieved for about two seconds. Then I realized I still had to get through lunch with Julia and Natasha. The whole walk from the band hall to the cafeteria, I racked my brain trying to think of something to talk about besides the chair test.

But before I even took out my sandwich, the perfect distraction walked by.

"Hi, Julia."

The three of us glanced up at Seth Anderson, and Julia immediately turned tomato red.

"Oh! Hi, um . . . Seth," she stammered, her voice unnaturally high.

The second he was out of earshot, Natasha and I started giggling uncontrollably.

"What?" Julia cried.

"You're *so red*!" I exclaimed. She glared at me, which only made me laugh harder. "And what's up with your voice?"

"'*Hi, um . . . Seth*,'" Natasha squeaked, grinning when Julia punched her lightly on the arm. "Did you actually forget his name or something? Or wait—were you trying to play it cool?"

"That's totally what it was," I said before Julia could respond. "She was all, do I know you? Wait, don't we have PE together or something?"

Natasha cracked up. "Hang on—*you're* the reason I got smacked in the face during dodgeball! I wasn't paying attention because I was too busy staring at your—"

"Okay, okay!" Julia was laughing despite herself. "Enough, guys. He just . . . surprised me. We've never actually talked before."

"It sounded like the first time you've ever *talked*, period," I said nonchalantly, unwrapping my sandwich. Julia groaned and buried her face in her hands, and Natasha and I grinned at each other.

For a second. Then we both realized what we were doing and looked away.

"*Any*way." Julia sat up, her cheeks still a little pink. "So, hey, I ended up getting fifth chair! Way better than I thought. But geez, you guys rocked it."

And we were back to awkward. I focused on opening my bag of chips, trying to look indifferent. "Thanks. I guess we're having another chair test in a few weeks, then?"

"Right before the football game," Natasha said quickly. "I hope Mr. Dante picks something a little harder. This one was way too easy, don't you think?" she added, giving me an innocent look.

I tossed my unopened bag of chips back into my lunch sack. "Yeah. Super easy." Glancing across the cafeteria, I scooted my chair back. "You know what? I totally forgot I need to talk to Owen about something. About, um, a science lab we have to do next period. I'll see you guys later, okay?"

Julia barely glanced up when I stood. "Yeah, okay. See you seventh."

Like she didn't even care.

"Can I sit with you?" I slumped down in the chair next to Owen before he could answer. Blinking, he set his Warlock cards down.

"Yeah, sure. Everything okay?"

"Everything's *great*." It came out more biting than I'd intended. "Sorry. Another bad day."

"Oh. Want to play?"

I glanced at Owen, then across the table. Trevor was sitting next to his lab partner, Brent the Nose Picker. I made a mental note not to touch any of his cards.

"Sure."

"Come on, seriously?" Trevor looked at me in disbelief. "You don't even know how to play!"

"I can figure it out," I snapped, taking my cards from Owen. Spreading them out in a fan, I studied them. "Um, Owen?" I mumbled, leaning toward him. "What the heck is a moonrat?"

I spent the rest of lunch trying to learn the rules of Warlock, which turned out to be insanely complicated. But Owen and Brent were pretty cool about it, and twenty minutes later, even Trevor was being nice. Kind of.

"Good one," he said approvingly when I tossed down a card with a goat-man. (Which was apparently called a satyr. Yes, I was learning the language of Geekdom.)

"Thanks." I collected a card from Brent (after checking for boogers), and Owen leaned over.

"If that was Trevor's card, he would've spilled his Coke on you and pretended it was an accident," he whispered, and I laughed.

"What is that?"

The four of us looked up just as a massive hand snatched up all of Trevor's cards. I froze. The red-haired giant. The one who was friends with . . .

Oh no. No no no no no.

"It's a goblin, dude. Oh man, this one says 'pixie,'" the giant snorted. "Check it out, Aaron. I got a pixie!" He waved the cards over Trevor's head.

At Aaron Cook.

Who was standing right there.

This was it. I was really, truly, seriously, honestly about to die in my chair, right here in the cafeteria. With Warlock cards in my hand.

"Knock it off, Rick." Aaron grabbed the cards from the giant's hands and gave them to Trevor. "Sorry. He's just being an idiot." Trevor mumbled something that sounded a lot like "What else is new." Lucky for him, Rick didn't appear to hear.

"Yeah, whatever. Come on, I need to hit the vending machines before fifth."

Rick the Giant lumbered off, but Aaron hesitated. I glanced up, and our eyes met.

Sorry, he mouthed. I shrugged and tried to smile.

He walked off just as the bell rang, and I stared numbly at the cards in my hand. *He didn't make fun of you,* I told myself. *Actually, he kind of defended you.*

But that only made me feel worse. Aaron was so nice. He was so nice *and* so cute. And now he thought I was a total geek.

I put my cards down and gathered my things slowly, not daring to look at Owen or anyone else. If I got through the rest of this day without crying, it'd be a miracle.

On Wednesday, I walked into the band hall feeling good. Sort of. Sure, Monday had been kind of rotten. But yesterday, Mr. Dante had handed out another new song—one we were going to perform at the football game. And it had a French horn solo.

The next chair test was after the pep rally, but before the game. Maybe Natasha had first chair for now, but I could get it next time. I *had* to. Because that would mean at the football game, I'd be playing that solo.

So long as I was passing science, of course. But I'd studied with Owen again yesterday after school, and we were meeting tomorrow, too.

Things might have gotten off to a rough start this year, but I was going to fix it.

I opened my horn case, feeling more confident than I had in weeks. When I straightened up and saw Aaron was at his cubby, I heard "Hey, Aaron," and briefly wondered who said it before I realized it was me. Okay, maybe I was feeling a little *too* confident.

He glanced over and smiled. "Hey, Holly. How's it going?"

"Great!" I smiled back at him and headed out into the band hall before my face had a chance to turn red. I was still fairly mortified that Aaron had seen me playing a dorky card game at lunch on Monday, but hey—he hadn't laughed or made fun of me. He'd even told Rick the Giant to stop.

"Hi, Gabby." I slipped past her and took my seat. "Hi, Natasha."

"Hey," they said in unison, Natasha looking mildly confused. I could smell Gabby's Red Hots breath from my chair. Opening my folder, I pulled out "Galactic March" and started reading through the horn solo, very aware of Natasha staring at me.

After we warmed up, Mr. Dante asked us to get the march out. We'd practiced it a little bit yesterday—it wasn't exactly easy, but nowhere near as hard as "Labyrinthine Dances." After playing the beginning a few times, he turned off the metronome.

"This time, let's go on and stop at measure sixty-two."

He counted us off, and we played. I'd practiced this part last night, so I already knew about the key change in measure forty-eight. At measure fifty-one, Mr. Dante glanced at the horns. When the band stopped, I turned to Natasha.

"There's a key change," I whispered loudly enough

for Mr. Dante to hear, pointing at her music. "I think you played a B-flat instead of a B in measure fifty-one."

"Holly's right—we're in the key of concert F now," Mr. Dante said, and I smiled sweetly. Natasha turned bright pink. "Trumpets, I heard a few wrong notes from you around there as well. Let's start right at measure forty-eight."

I sat up straight, trying not to look too pleased. I could practically feel Natasha's glare.

A few minutes later, Mr. Dante asked the horns and saxes to play four measures together. When we finished, he glanced down at his score.

"Play just measure fifty-nine, and when you get to the third note, hold it until I stop you."

We did, and I heard it—we were out of tune. Mr. Dante asked each of us to play the note one at a time. After I played, Natasha cleared her throat.

"It might help if you adjust your hand," she said brightly, turning to me so I could see the angle of her hand in the bell of her horn. "Try it like this."

I forced myself to smile back, even though inside I wanted to scream. "Thanks! I will."

Five minutes later, she skipped a rest and I immediately pointed it out. And just a minute after that, I missed a note and she showed me the fingering. By the end of class, my cheeks felt sore from fake-smiling and I was definitely reaching new levels of apoplectic. I took longer than necessary to put my music in my folder, while Natasha practically sprinted to her cubby.

"What was that about?" Gabby asked. She was still in her chair, looking at me curiously.

"What was what about?"

"You and Natasha. I thought for sure one of you was going to slap the other before rehearsal was over."

I glanced around. Julia was already in the cubby room, putting her clarinet away and chatting with Sophie Wheeler. "Why would you think that?" I said innocently. "We were just . . . helping each other."

Gabby snorted. "Yeah. If you say so."

𝄞

"Which type of organelle creates energy for a cell?"

"Um . . ." My eyes strayed to the stack of cards on the coffee table. Owen sat facing me on the couch, his textbook open in his lap. At my feet, Worf gnawed on a piece of rawhide. I chewed my lip, thinking. "Mitochondria?"

"Right!" he exclaimed, and I let out a breath of relief. I'd definitely gotten the hang of our game, but as soon as Owen had decided to quiz me, panic set in. The science test was Monday, and it definitely wasn't going to involve cards with goofy pictures on them.

"How many have I gotten right so far?" I asked, and Owen checked his notebook.

"Fourteen out of twenty."

I slumped into the cushion, and Worf leaped onto my lap. "Stellar."

"It's passing," Owen said.

"Barely." I sat up quickly. "Not that this hasn't—I mean, you've helped me a ton! It's definitely much better than my quiz grade. I just . . . I can't risk failing it at all."

"You won't fail."

Worf started chewing my finger as I watched Owen gather up the cards and twist a rubber band around them. I wished I was as confident in myself as he apparently was. "Here, take these. You can use them over the weekend to study."

"Thanks." I slipped the cards into my backpack, then glanced at the clock. "So . . . *Prophets?*"

Owen grinned. *"Prophets."*

I handed Worf over to him, then got up to find the disc and hook up the controllers. Behind the stack of shoe boxes sat a squat, wide shelf filled with DVDs. I flipped through a few.

"*Dark Planet, Project Centaurus . . .*" I turned around, eyebrows raised. "*Cyborgs versus Ninjas?*"

"*Cyborgs versus Ninjas*," Owen said solemnly, "is the greatest movie ever made."

I tried not to laugh as I tossed him a controller and flopped back on the couch. "No way. Not possible. I saw the greatest movie ever made last weekend. It just came out."

"Holly, I swear if you say *Seven Dates* I'm never inviting you over again."

I snorted. "Gross, no way. It was *House of the Wicked*."

Owen blinked in surprise. "Seriously, you went to see that?"

"My brother took me. It was *amazing*." I leaned forward, pushing my controller aside. "It's about this guy and his daughter who move into this old house, and the girl starts seeing all this crazy stuff. Like her toys—she keeps finding them in weird places. All her dolls disappear and she finds their eyes in the ice tray in the freezer, and her jump rope gets twisted up in the ceiling fan, stuff like that. Oh my God, and at this one part she goes into the bathroom and the mirror is covered in—" I stopped, because Owen was laughing at me. "What?"

"You like horror movies?"

"Most movies that *aren't* horror are boring," I said flatly. "They're all predictable. But horror movies—not the gory ones, I mean the ones that are scary without blood and guts—it's almost impossible to figure out the ending. You would *never* guess the ending of *House*."

Owen looked skeptical. "Not *all* other types of movies are predictable."

"Yes they are. Doesn't matter if it's romance or action or sci-fi—no offense—they've all got a good guy and a bad guy, and the good guy pretty much always wins. You know the ending before the movie's halfway done."

"And horror movies don't have good guys and bad guys?"

"Sometimes, but it doesn't matter." I shifted as Worf climbed back into my lap. "They can trick you. Maybe the bad guy wins, or maybe the one you thought was good was bad. Or maybe everyone dies. Or maybe everyone was dead the whole time. They're always different."

Owen considered this. "Want to make a bet?" he said finally.

"A bet?"

He nodded. "I'll bet you can't guess the ending of *Cyborgs versus Ninjas*."

I started laughing. "Owen, that's stupid! Either one wins or the other. Cyborgs or ninjas. I've got a fifty-fifty chance."

"No, I mean you should watch it," Owen said, "and halfway through, you tell me the ending."

"Easy." I glanced at the clock. "Not today, though—I have to be home in half an hour."

"Sure." Owen started scrolling through the *Prophets* menu, then glanced at me. "No looking up the ending online, though."

I snorted. "Please. I won't have to."

We played for twenty minutes, and I killed twelve aliens and blew up two pods. Secretly, I was looking forward to the next time Trevor came over. He wouldn't be making fun of me again.

When I got into the car, Mom held up a plastic bag with a flourish.

"Ta-da! I stopped by the mall after work today."

"Ooh, what is it?" I squealed, grabbing the bag and turning it over. Shiny blue fabric spilled out onto my lap. "*Wow.*"

It was dress. A *gorgeous* dress. Light blue, capped sleeves, with a thin black belt and a black flower pattern along the bottom.

"Mom!" I yelled excitedly. "I have boots that would go perfect with this!"

"I know!" she yelled back.

"Thank you!"

"You're welcome!"

We hugged. I examined the dress up close. "What's this for, anyway?"

"The band party, dork," said Mom, checking her rearview mirror and pulling away from the curb. "Next Friday, right?"

"Oh . . . right, yeah."

Mom gave me a strange look. "Are you okay, Holly?"

"What?" I looked up. "Yeah, I'm fine."

"Okay."

I turned my attention back to the dress, but my excitement had definitely faded. Depending on how Monday went, there was a chance I wouldn't even get to wear it.

I called Julia twice on Saturday and she never called back. So Chad and I watched all three *Watch the Fog* movies, and then he went out with his friends and I did nothing.

On Sunday, Dad took us to the lake. As usual, he and Chad ignored me every time I told them to put on more sunblock. And as usual, by the time we got home they were both practically purple.

"Ice," groaned Chad, lumbering like a zombie over to the freezer. He grabbed a bag of frozen chicken nuggets and held it to the back of his neck. I rolled my eyes.

Dad headed into the laundry room with a bag full of wet towels and bathing suits. "Holly, will you check the messages?"

"Sure." I walked to the phone as Chad rubbed the bag of nuggets on his face.

"Chad, gross!" Mom appeared in the doorway, arms

crossed. "Next time just listen to your sister and put on the sunblock."

I smiled smugly at Chad, and he stuck his tongue out.

When I pressed play on the answering machine, it beeped once. "Hey, Holly, it's Julia. Call me back!"

"Let me know when you're off the phone," Mom said as I hurried up to my room.

"Okay!" I yelled back. But when I closed my door, I pulled Owen's cards out of my backpack without even looking at my phone. It wasn't that I didn't *want* to talk to Julia. But my stomach was starting to knot up about this test tomorrow, and I figured a last-minute cram session couldn't hurt.

And anyway, maybe I would call Julia back if she'd bothered to return my call yesterday. But she hadn't, so I wasn't going to, either.

The knots got tighter and tighter all Monday morning. By the time band rolled around, I was too anxious to think of a retort when Natasha cattily pointed out a tiny rhythm mistake I made in the march. At lunch, I got through half my sandwich before giving up and shoving everything back into the sack.

And then I was at my desk, listening to Mrs. Driscoll tell us to get out our pencils and put everything else away. I shuffled through the cards one last time, and Owen smiled at me.

"Good luck!"

"Thanks, Owen."

Mrs. Driscoll handed me the test—three pages, holy cow—and I took a deep breath. *Here we go.*

1. Centrioles are found in:

A) plant cells

B) animal cells

C) both

D) neither

I pictured the blade chopping the onion and grinned, my stomach knots loosening a tiny bit. Maybe this wouldn't be so bad.

𝄞

I got to first-period English ten minutes early on Tuesday. Gabby was already there, ripping open a bag of M&M's.

"M&M's for breakfast, Red Hots for lunch?" I asked, tossing my bag down on the desk in front of hers.

"The Red Hots aren't my *lunch*, Holly," Gabby said around a mouthful of chocolate. "They're to help me not starve to death *before* lunch." She swallowed, then gave me an innocent look. "Lunch is peanut butter cups."

I laughed, then swiveled around when Mr. Franks entered the room. My eyes zeroed in on the packet in his hand.

Progress reports.

"I really hope he hands them out at the beginning

of class." I didn't even realize I'd spoken out loud until Gabby responded.

"You worried?"

I turned away from Mr. Franks. "No, not *worried*. Just, um . . . curious."

Yeah, right. Curious. There was no way I could make it till the end of class without knowing my grade in science. By the time the bell rang, I had a half-formed plan that involved asking to go the bathroom, distracting Mr. Franks by knocking over his coffee, and stealing that packet.

Fortunately, I didn't have to resort to that.

"When I call your name, please come get your progress report."

While Mr. Franks called the first lucky half of the alphabet, I stared at my desk and went through the science test in my head. Yesterday, I'd felt pretty good about it—there'd been a lot of questions I knew the answers to for sure. But now, all I could focus on were the ones I hadn't known. And after a minute, I'd pretty much convinced myself that all the ones I was positive I'd gotten right were totally wrong, too. When Mr. Franks finally said, "Holly Mead," I'd all but accepted that I failed.

I walked up to the front, took my progress report without looking at it, then sat back in my chair. Fingers shaking, I spread it out on my desk and looked.

Science (5th, Driscoll): 80

I stared at the number hard, as if it were going to change right in front of my eyes. Eighty. *Eighty.* That wasn't just passing, it was a B! Still the lowest grade I'd ever gotten on a progress report, but the relief was so great it felt like I was floating.

I pretty much checked out for the rest of class. In my head, I was at the band party wearing my new dress. By the end of third period, I'd even worked up the nerve to have a real conversation with Aaron. I was so distracted that when I walked into the band hall it took me a minute to notice Julia talking to Mr. Dante by his office.

She was crying.

I hovered there for a second, torn between rushing over to her and not wanting to interrupt. Finally, I ran to my cubby and got my horn out as fast as I could. When I left the cubby room, Mr. Dante was back in his office. Julia was over in the corner with Natasha, wiping her eyes.

I hurried over to them. "What happened?"

Julia sniffled and wordlessly handed me a piece of paper—her progress report. I scanned it, and my eyes widened.

History (1st, Peterson): 64

Oh no.

"Mr. Dante said I can still play during rehearsal," she whispered. "But not at the pep rally. If I'm passing on my report card, I'll at least be able to play at the football game, though."

"I'm really sorry, Julia." I didn't know what else to say. Natasha just stood there, staring at the floor. Glancing back at the progress report, I realized history was one of the classes they had together. Natasha had probably known for weeks that Julia was having trouble with history.

"I don't know what to do, though," Julia went on. "I passed the first quiz, but the second one was way harder. I've been going in for tutoring in the morning, but we had a test last week and I just . . ." Her voice broke. "I don't know if I'll even be able to pass on my report card."

Suddenly, I wanted to kick myself. This whole time Julia had been acting so weird, I'd thought she was upset with me. But she'd been worried about history, just like I'd been stressing over science. She hadn't been avoiding me before school—she was going to history early to get help.

I gave her a hug. "You're going to pass," I said firmly. "Maybe you can't go to the pep rally, but you're definitely coming to that football game with us. Okay?"

"Okay." Julia smiled briefly, then it faltered. "But still, Friday . . ." My stomach dropped as I realized what she meant.

Julia couldn't go to the band party.

Since Owen and I weren't studying after school, I took the bus home. I walked in and went straight upstairs and into my room and lay facedown on my bed. Almost an hour later, Mom called me from downstairs, jolting me awake.

I trudged into the kitchen. "Hi."

"Help me put the groceries away?" she asked. Nodding, I grabbed a plastic bag and started pulling out chicken and tomatoes and sour cream. "I thought I'd try making fajitas tonight," she said cheerfully, and I burst into tears.

"Holly? What is it?"

She sat across from me at the table, looking concerned. I pulled my progress report out of my pocket and handed it to her. Scanning it, she fixed me with a stern glare.

"Holly, if you're actually getting this upset about an eighty, we need to have a serious talk."

"No, it's not that." I wiped my face on my sleeve. "Actually, I'm happy about it. I, um . . . I actually failed my first quiz in science. Like, mega-failed."

Mom raised an eyebrow. "Did you go in for tutoring?"

"Well, not exactly," I said. "But . . . you know how I've been going to Owen's house after school? He's been helping me—we're lab partners. And I had a test yesterday, and I passed."

Sitting back in her chair, Mom pursed her lips like she was trying not to laugh. "Wow, what a horror story. I can see why you're so upset."

I rolled my eyes. "It's not that. I'm upset because . . . well, you know Mr. Dante's rule? If you're failing a class, you can't participate in band stuff. And Julia . . . she's failing history." The tears started welling up again, and I swallowed. "So she can't go to the party this Friday, or play at the pep rally. Maybe not even at the football game."

Mom nodded slowly. "That's a shame. I'm really sorry, I know how much you're looking forward to the party. It won't be the same without Julia." She paused for a moment. "But, Holly, what's really bugging you?"

"What do you mean?"

Sighing, Mom stood and started putting away the groceries. "You know exactly what I mean. Since school started, I haven't seen Julia over here once, and you haven't been over there. Sunday night when she called you, you didn't call back—yes, I noticed," she added. "What's the deal?"

So I told her. Mom put away cans of beans and tortillas and shredded cheese, and I sat there and talked about everything. Seeing Natasha on the first day of school with Julia. How they'd met at band camp. How Julia had kissed some guy named Garrett and hadn't even told me. How she'd invited Natasha to the movies before me. How Natasha had beat me for first chair in band.

"She's just . . . stealing *everything* from me." My voice sounded thick, and I was relieved Chad hadn't come downstairs yet. "I don't know why Julia likes her so much."

Mom closed the fridge and sat down. "Done?"

I nodded. "Yeah."

"Okay." Mom clasped her hands on the table. "Holly, I don't think the question is why Julia likes Natasha. I think the question is, why don't you?"

I stared at her. "Why don't I *like* her?" I sputtered. "Okay, for one thing, she's totally stuck-up. She never shuts up about herself, how *easy* her classes are, how *easy* our band music is, how *good* she is on the stupid debate team. And, oh my God, and she cuts her sandwich with a knife and fork, it's so stupid. And she—"

Mom shook her head, laughing. "Okay, okay. Maybe you're right—although keep in mind, this girl just started at a new school, and Julia was the only friend she had. So maybe you should cut her a little slack. She might not be as bad as you think."

Yeah, right. I didn't say that out loud, but I knew Mom knew I was thinking it.

"Okay, never mind about Natasha," she said. "What about Julia? You say she's been acting distant, but haven't you been doing the same to her?"

When I opened my mouth, I was going to say no. But I couldn't. Because as much as I hated to admit it, Mom was right. I didn't go to Julia's locker in the morning anymore. I hadn't called her back last weekend. I said no to the movie and to fajitas. I hadn't worn the turtle necklace in over a week. And I couldn't even be upset that she hadn't told me about failing history, because I hadn't told her about failing science.

Mom glanced at the clock. "Dinner's at six thirty," she said, standing up. "Plenty of time to go over there and talk to her now, if you want to."

"Okay." I stood, still sniffling. "Thanks, Mom."

She smiled at me. "Anytime."

Julia's house was a fifteen-minute walk from mine. By the time I knocked on the door, I'd worked out what I wanted to say. Sort of.

"Well, hey, stranger!" Mr. Gordon stepped back to let me in, smiling broadly. "Feels like I haven't seen you in ages!"

"Hi, Mr. Gordon," I said. "Is Julia home?"

"Yup, she's in her room." He lowered his voice. "You have history with Julia, right?"

"No, sir."

"Ah." His smiled faded. "Well, she's pretty upset about her progress report—and so am I. Julia's never failed a class before."

"I know," I said. "But she can still pass on her report card. She will, I know it."

Mr. Gordon nodded. "I'm sure she will."

The door to Julia's room was open a crack. I knocked twice and pushed it open. She was sprawled out on her bed, earphones in, magazine open.

She didn't notice me come in. Not until I grabbed her foot, anyway. Then she screamed loud enough to rival any horror-movie star and chucked the magazine across the room.

I sank down on her bed, laughing. "Sorry, couldn't help it."

"Jeez, Holly!" Julia sat up, ripping the earphones out. "Give me a heart attack."

"Sorry," I said again. But I couldn't stop giggling, and she threw a pillow at me.

"What are you doing here?"

I held the pillow in my lap, twirling the fringe around my fingers. "I just wanted to see how you're doing. I'm really sorry about the history thing."

Julia sighed. "It's my fault. I just . . . I don't know. I tried to study, but the book is so. Boring."

"I know what you mean," I admitted. "I kind of almost failed science, too."

"Really?" She looked surprised. "You didn't tell me that."

"Yeah. I got really behind on the first day and it just got worse from there." I glanced up at her. "I failed this one quiz, and Mrs. Driscoll said I had to pass this test we had yesterday to pass on my progress report."

"Yikes," said Julia. "But you did, obviously."

"Only because Owen helped me. I've been going over to his place after school to study."

"Oh."

"He really helped me a ton." I hesitated, thinking. I really didn't want to suggest this, but Julia passing history was more important than everything else. "Isn't there someone in your history class that can help you? Isn't . . . isn't Natasha in that class?"

Julia examined a fingernail. "Yeah, she is. But I . . ." She stopped, then shook her head.

"What?"

"Nothing," she said. "Anyway, I can't believe I'm not going to the party Friday."

So apparently she didn't want to talk about Natasha. I turned my attention back to the pillow fringe. "I know. I don't even want to go without you."

Julia laughed sadly. "You have to, though. Maybe something will happen with Aaron."

Heat flushed my face, and I stared at her. "What do you mean?"

Now she was laughing for real. "Oh, come on, Holly. I know you."

I smiled despite myself. "Yeah, I guess you do." Then I threw the pillow at her. "And by the way, how could you not tell me his locker is right next to yours?"

She grinned. "Why, did you talk to him?"

"As a matter of fact, he talked to me first." I sat up

straight. "*And*, he said he liked my necklace. The turtle one you gave me."

"Really?" Julia said. "Guess you owe me one, huh?"

"Guess so." I smiled, suddenly feeling better than I had in weeks. She was smiling, too. Then it faded.

"I've got to pass history. Maybe I have to miss the party, but I can't miss the football game, too."

"You'll pass," I said firmly. "I'll help you."

"Me too."

We both looked up in surprise.

Natasha stood in the doorway, light blue backpack slung around her shoulder.

"Hey!" Julia sat up. "I didn't know you were coming over."

"We've got a history quiz Friday." Natasha dropped her bag on the bed and unzipped it, giving me a sickeningly sweet smile. "And Holly's right—you're going to pass." She pulled out her textbook. "I got a hundred on our last quiz—I know I can help you."

It took massive effort not to roll my eyes. *Why don't you rub it in a little*. I hopped off the bed.

"You're leaving?"

The look on Julia's face was hard to read. Not angry, but disappointed, confused . . . maybe hurt?

I tried to sound normal. "Yeah, Mom's making dinner." Pausing in the doorway, I watched Natasha flip open her notebook. "Good luck, Julia."

"Thanks!" said Natasha, giving me her biggest fake-smile yet. Julia's smile was much smaller.

"Thanks, Holly," she said quietly.

On the walk home, I focused hard on counting the number of rocks I kicked. My eyes were dry by the time I got home.

On Friday morning, I got to school absurdly early and headed straight to Julia's locker. The night before, Mom and I had stayed up late making a couple of dozen origami four-leaf clovers, which were now in the grocery bag that I was setting down on the floor to spin her combination.

Five minutes and about half a roll of tape later, I stepped back to survey my handiwork and grinned. The clovers (which were covered in green glitter) spelled out *good luck* on the inside of the door. She'd see it right before history class.

Smiling to myself, I shut her locker and jumped about a foot in the air when I realized someone was on the other side of it.

"Hey, Holly." Aaron glanced at me from his locker and laughed. "Did I scare you? You looked pretty focused on whatever you were doing in there."

I tried to catch my breath, which, let's face it, was

a losing battle. "Yeah, I was, um . . . leaving my friend Julia a note."

"Ah." He went back to digging through his locker, which was kind of a wreck. I took the opportunity to admire his profile, which, in contrast, was very well put-together. "Do you know what time it is?"

"Seven fifty-eight," I said promptly. Aaron groaned.

"I'm gonna be late for practice." Straightening up, he shoved back a cascading mess of papers and notebooks, then slammed the door shut. It was going to be, like, a total avalanche next time he opened it. Glancing at the clock, Aaron crammed two books into his backpack and zipped it. "You going to the band party tonight?"

Breathe, Holly. Inhale.

"Yes! Um . . . yeah. Are you?"

"Yeah." He smiled at me, and somehow I didn't fall over. (The smile parentheses. They hurt.) "Guess I'll see you there."

"That's . . . um, right. You will. See me, I mean."

As soon as he disappeared around the corner, I leaned against the lockers and sank to the floor. Fifty-one minutes until first period started. Maybe I could use the time to try to remember how to speak like a normal human being.

𝄞

"Seventy-two." Julia took her reed out of her mouth and placed it on her mouthpiece. "Not enough to change my overall grade, but it's way better than my last quiz," she added, sliding on the ligature.

"If you do okay on the next quiz and get a B on the test the week after that, you'll pass," said Natasha. "I'll make more flash cards this weekend."

"Thanks," Julia replied, then smiled at me. "And thanks again for the good-luck-wish decorations this morning, Holly."

I grinned. "I guess they worked!"

"Yup!" Her smile suddenly looked devious. "Although I can't help but wonder if there's another reason you wanted to spend all morning at my locker."

"Shh!" I glanced around, giggling, but Aaron wasn't there yet. "I have no idea what you're talking about."

"Yeah, right." Julia lowered her voice. "So did you talk to him again?"

"Talk to who?" Natasha's tone was cheerful, but she looked vaguely irritated. It made me happier than I cared to admit.

"No one," I said quickly, picking my horn up. Julia just grinned as we headed to our seats.

Chair test number two was in less than two weeks. This time, the test was on a chorale we did during warm-ups that was actually kind of hard. Maybe I had to be fake nice to Natasha, but my days of second chair were done. As soon as I sat down, I started reading through the part we were being tested on for the fifth time, pushing down the valves and tapping my foot.

"Cute!"

I glanced over and saw Gabby pointing at Natasha's shoes as she sat down. (Purple plaid ballet flats. Okay, they *were* pretty cute. I had a dress they'd look great with.)

"Thanks!" Natasha said. "Early birthday present from my aunt."

"Nice!" Gabby replied. "When's your birthday?"

"Saturday after next." Natasha's voice got louder all of a sudden. "Actually, I'm having a party—you should come!"

I stopped mid-measure, fingers frozen over the valves.

"I'd love to!" Gabby said. "That's the day after the football game, yeah?"

"Yup."

I wasn't looking at her, but I could hear that smug smile in Natasha's voice. Mr. Dante saved me from further torment when he stepped onto the podium. But I had a hard time focusing on the warm-ups.

A party. All my friends would be invited, and I wouldn't. Stellar.

The more I thought about it, the harder it was to stick with the whole "be fake nice to Natasha" thing. While we rehearsed "Galactic March," I kept picturing Julia and Gabby and everyone at her house, giving her presents and having fun without me. So when we got to the horn solo and I heard Natasha whisper to Gabby, "I wish this solo was our chair test next week instead of the chorale. It's so easy!" I was pretty much done.

I sat rigidly in my chair, waiting until Mr. Dante finished talking to the low brass. "Let's start right at the horn solo, measure ninety-two," he said, lifting his hands.

I kept my horn in my lap, staring at Natasha's feet while she played. She sounded great, which only fueled my anger. Discreetly, I lifted my horn to my lips and leaned over and to the side just a little bit. Blowing air into the mouthpiece, I pushed down the spit valve.

Bull's-eye.

I leaned back in my chair, trying not to smile. Of course, it was a shame to ruin such an adorable pair of shoes. But I felt *so* much better.

For a second. Then I saw Gabby looking right at me, and my stomach dropped. She looked surprised . . . and disappointed.

Whatever. I lifted my horn again, ready to come in with Brooke and Owen after the solo. It wasn't *that* big a deal, right? Natasha's shoes couldn't be *totally* ruined. And she deserved it.

"Holly."

I looked up at Mr. Dante, and my insides instantly turned to ice.

He'd seen me.

I swallowed hard. "Yes?" *Oh God oh God oh God.*

He was silent for a few seconds, looking at me with this mix of disappointment and shock that made me want to go hole up in my cubby for the rest of my life. Before he could speak, Natasha shrieked.

"My shoe! What the heck is that?" She stuck her foot out, then stared at me, her mouth open. "Did you empty your *spit valve* on my *shoe?*"

Oh God.

Sophie Wheeler squealed in disgust, and behind me, a few of the boys laughed. I could feel Julia staring at me. On the other side of Natasha, Gabby's eyes were glued to the floor. My face burned.

"Holly?" Mr. Dante said again.

I cleared my throat, but my voice came out all shaky and weak anyway. "It was an accident."

Could I have said anything more lame? Probably not. Natasha just gaped at me, her leg still extended as if she was trying to get as far away from her own foot as humanly possible.

Mr. Dante studied me thoughtfully. He knew I was lying, I could tell. I shifted in my chair.

"Then I suggest you be more careful in the future," he said at last. "And I believe you owe Natasha an apology."

I thought nothing could be more humiliating than Aaron Cook seeing me playing Warlock with a bunch of nerds. Clearly, I was wrong.

"Sorry," I mumbled, turning toward Natasha but not meeting her eyes.

"Okay," she said. But as soon as Mr. Dante started rehearsal again, I saw her and Sophie exchange a Look.

Oh my God, Sophie mouthed at her, and Natasha snickered. Sophie made a disgusted face at me before turning back around in her chair.

When rehearsal finally ended (like, a decade later), I just stayed in my chair with my eyes fixed on my folder, trying to not look guilty. Trevor didn't help by jabbing me in the arm with his trombone slide, causing me to jump about a foot off my chair.

"What?" I yelped. He grinned at me.

"Good one."

"Huh?"

Trevor looked pointedly at Natasha, who was making a big show of wiping her shoe with a rag. "I did that to Max in beginner class all the time when he got annoying." He headed to the cubby room, and I stared after him in shock.

I was officially as immature as Trevor Wells. This had to be rock-bottom, right?

"Holly, I need to speak with you in my office, please."

Wrong.

I couldn't even look up at Mr. Dante. Leaving my horn on my chair, I followed him to the front of the band hall without taking my eyes off my shoes.

Inside his office, he closed the door, then leaned against his desk. But he didn't say anything. I fidgeted, staring at the spreadsheet opened on his computer monitor. This was one of my mom's tactics, too—waiting and waiting until the silence was just too much and I confessed to whatever it was I was trying to pretend I hadn't done.

It drove me nuts, because it always worked.

"I'm really sorry!" I burst out after five seconds of unbearably awkward silence. "I don't know why I did that. I mean, I *do* know why I did it, but I know I shouldn't have done it, you know?"

Mr. Dante arched an eyebrow. "And why exactly did you do it?"

"Because . . ." I trailed off, staring at my shoes again. Somehow *Because Natasha was being a total jerk* didn't seem like an answer Mr. Dante would appreciate.

I cleared my throat. "I, um . . . I don't get along very well with Natasha."

"And?"

Confused, I glanced up. "And what?"

Mr. Dante shrugged. "You seem like a pretty sensible girl, Holly. Do you really think not getting along with someone is a reason to empty your spit valve on her shoe?"

My face grew hot. "No," I said in a small voice.

"I didn't think so. You know, Mrs. Wendell told me a lot about you this summer."

I blinked in surprise. "Really?"

"Yup." Pulling open his top desk drawer, Mr. Dante pulled out a notebook and began flipping through the labels. The *color-coded* labels—nice. "I took notes when I met with her after I was hired," he added when he saw me staring, and I tried to smile.

"Oh."

"Here we go—sixth-graders, French horn." Mr.

Dante tapped the page. "She said you were very talented, well-behaved, one of her best and most hardworking students . . . and apparently you had a knack for making great concert programs?"

I blushed again, but for a different reason this time.

"So." Mr. Dante closed his notebook. "How does such a responsible, mature student go from this"—he held up the notebook—"to what I saw from you today?"

I squeezed my eyes shut. Oh my God, this guy could even give Mom a run for her money for the title of Guilt Trip Master.

What could I say? *Because Natasha is having a birthday party and probably not inviting me. Because she stole my best friend. Because she got first chair instead of me—which is* totally *unfair, by the way.*

Nope. Not about to say that to Mr. Dante.

"I don't know," I said at last, opening my eyes. "I . . . I really am sorry, Mr. Dante. It won't happen again, ever. I've never done anything so—so *gross* before. Seriously, it's something my brother would do," I added with a shudder. Mr. Dante chuckled, and I smiled weakly in relief.

"Glad to hear it, Holly. Thank you." Opening the top drawer, he placed the notebook back inside. The score to "Labyrinthine Dances" was open on his desk. I leaned forward a little, my eyes widening.

"Did you . . . did you *color* this?"

Mr. Dante nodded, flipping a few pages so I could see. "I just highlight certain things so I can see them at a glance. Dynamics are green, tempo changes are orange, key changes are blue . . . you get the idea."

Whoa. The man was a genius.

"You'd better get to lunch, Holly. And listen . . ." I tore my eyes off the beauty of the color-coded score and looked at him. "I appreciate your apology, and I know you mean it. But you need to tell Natasha you're sorry." Adjusting his glasses again, Mr. Dante smiled. "I know she . . . pushes your buttons sometimes. But, Holly, you push hers, too, and you know it. And like it or not, you're going to be in the same section for the rest of the year. Seems like the best thing to do would be at least *try* to get along, right?"

I nodded fervently. "Yes, sir."

Back out in the empty band hall, I grabbed my horn and hurried to the cubby room. I meant what I said to Mr. Dante, sort of. No way was I going to try to be friends with Natasha—that was a lost cause. But I'd definitely try to pretend to get along with her during band if it would make Mr. Dante happy. Mrs. Wendell had told him I was one of her best students, and I was going to start acting like it.

I was also going to start color-coding my music, like, immediately.

Outside the band hall doors, a voice interrupted my mental music highlighting.

"So what *was* that?"

Startled, I turned to see Julia leaning against the wall.

"Oh! You scared me," I said lightly, but she didn't smile. Actually, she looked pretty upset.

Uh-oh.

"What *was* that in there?" she asked again. I shifted my weight from one foot to the other.

"Um, what was what?"

Julia rolled her eyes. "You know exactly what. Did you seriously *spit* on Natasha's shoes on purpose?"

"I didn't *spit* on them," I said defensively. "I—it was from my horn, and—"

"Whatever." Julia's arms were tightly crossed over her chest. "So was it on purpose?"

I waited a second too long to respond. My stomach dropped at the look on her face.

"Oh my *God*, Holly." Julia closed her eyes briefly. "I mean . . . why would you do that?"

I swallowed hard, but it wasn't enough to stop the lump rising in my throat.

"I don't know," I said at last, my voice all wobbly and weird. "I wasn't thinking, I was just . . . I was upset."

"Why?" She said it flatly; no sympathy. I took a deep breath and thought about what Mr. Dante said.

"Because Natasha kind of . . . pushes my buttons. Sometimes."

"What?"

"Come *on*, Julia," I cried, exasperated. "You can't seriously be this blind. She's awful! She's full of herself, she's obnoxious, she's constantly talking about—"

"Holly!" Julia was gaping at me. "Look, I just left the cafeteria because Natasha and Sophie were bad-mouthing *you*. But I'm not going to stand here and listen to you say all this stuff about Natasha, either!"

"But what *I'm* saying is actually true!" I said, my eyes burning with tears. "She's—"

"No, what *they're* saying is true," Julia snapped. "That you were so jealous of Natasha that you actually dumped spit on her shoes. Right?"

"Jealous?" I wiped my eyes furiously. "I'm not jealous—see, she thinks she's—"

"Really? You're not jealous she got first chair?"

I just stood there, mouth open.

This was unreal. It's not like Julia and I had never fought before . . . but it was never anything like this. And she was actually *defending Natasha*.

"Look, Holly." Julia's eyes were watery, too, but her voice was firm. "I told Natasha and Sophie I thought it was an accident. I told them you'd never do anything so disgusting. And I'm not going to listen to Natasha say things like that about you, ever."

When I didn't reply, she continued.

"But I'm not going to listen to *you* talk about Natasha like that, either. She's my friend, too, Holly. And I . . ." Julia looked away for a second. "I just can't deal with the two of you . . . being like this."

I stared at the linoleum, Julia's words ringing in my ears.

She's my friend, too, Holly.

Never mind the third-grade talent show, the countless sleepovers, the four years of best friendship. Two weeks with Natasha at Lake Lindon had been enough. It didn't matter that the girl clearly hated me—Julia still considered her a friend.

So what did that make me?

"Fine," I said at last. "But you know what, Julia? She's not *my* friend. And if hanging out with her is that important to you, maybe you should just do it without me."

Julia looked surprised for a second, then her mouth set in a firm line.

"Fine."

"Fine."

Turning, I headed to the bathroom without looking back.

By the time Mom dropped me off at Spins for the band party, it was already pretty crowded. I hovered in the entrance, looking for familiar faces. Spins was part pizza buffet, part arcade, and it was kind of dimly lit. There were definitely a lot of advanced-band members here already, and I recognized a bunch of seventh-graders who were in symphonic band. There were several kids I didn't recognize, but judging from their height, I figured they were in beginner band. (Seriously, was I that short in sixth grade?)

Mr. Dante was in a booth chatting with the parent chaperones. For, like, the millionth time, I thought about Julia sitting at home and tried to push the image out of my mind. I couldn't believe I'd yelled at her like that after band. At the same time, I was still a little too hurt by what she'd said to call her (although I'd picked up the phone without dialing about a dozen times before leaving for Spins).

Ignoring yet another wave of guilt, I spotted Gabby and a few girls by the drinks. I started heading their way, then stopped.

By the time I'd gotten home from school, I'd convinced myself that what happened during band wasn't that big of a deal. But now . . . Half the kids in this room had been there to witness my humiliation. I edged back toward the doors, a blush heating my cheeks. I couldn't face everyone. Maybe I should just quit band and join the choir or something. My singing voice wasn't bad.

Then I shook my head. I was being ridiculous. Like I would ever do choir.

"Hey, Holly!" Gabby waved, holding a plate piled high with cinnamon breadsticks from the buffet in her other hand. Next to her, Victoria Rios, a trumpet player, and Leah Collins, a percussionist, were eating slices of pizza. Taking a deep breath, I headed over.

"Hey," I said nervously. Gabby smiled at me.

"Love your dress."

Inwardly, I sighed in relief. She wasn't going to mention the spit-valve thing.

"Thanks!" I couldn't help but stare at Gabby's plate. "Seriously, do you ever eat anything but sweet stuff?"

"Nope," Victoria answered immediately. "One time in fifth grade I dared her to eat a pickle at lunch because she'd never had one."

"You were in fifth grade the first time you ate a *pickle?*" Leah exclaimed, picking the olives off her pizza.

Gabby nodded, swallowing. "Yup. Vic bet me a week's worth of chocolate pudding that I couldn't eat the whole thing. So I did. Then I puked. Totally worth it."

We laughed. "You can't blame her for all the candy, though," Victoria added. "You should see the food situation at her house."

"What do you mean?" I asked, and Gabby's eyes widened.

"My mom is *insane*," she said emphatically. "There is, like, zero sugar in our kitchen. And, oh my God, the stuff I have to eat for dinner. You would *die*."

I giggled. "It can't be *that* bad." But she and Victoria both shook their heads.

"Holly, you know what my mom made for dinner last night?" Gabby paused, wrinkling her nose. "Tofu lentil casserole and beet salad."

Leah and I looked at each other. "Okay, that sounds pretty gross," Leah admitted.

"And I have to drink carrot juice with wheatgrass every morning before school." Gabby pointed her cinnamon stick at each of us in turn. "Any of you ever tasted wheatgrass?" We shook our heads. "Pick a bunch of grass from your front yard and stick it in a blender with some carrots. *That's* what it tastes like."

I made a disgusted face. Suddenly Gabby's Red Hots obsession was making a lot of sense.

"Hey, there's Natasha!" Leah said suddenly.

I glanced up, heart pounding. Natasha was

standing alone at the entrance, apparently oblivious to Leah's frantic waving. Squinting, I realized her dress was a lot like mine. Too much like mine. It was pink instead of blue, and the little belt was brown instead of black, but other than that they were almost identical. Ugh, she was even wearing boots kind of like mine.

"Gonna spit on those boots, too?"

Alarmed, I stared at Victoria, but she was laughing. "What? No!" I cried, the stomach knots back in full force.

"Oh, leave her alone, Victoria," Leah said, smiling at me. "Holly wouldn't do that on purpose! That was an accident, right?"

"Right." I smiled back shakily. Gabby gave me a sideways look, cramming an entire cinnamon stick into her mouth. As soon as Leah and Victoria started talking to a few guys getting sodas, Gabby leaned closer to me.

"Okay, so what's up with you and Natasha? Seriously."

"Oh, just . . . nothing."

Choosing another cinnamon stick, Gabby rolled her eyes. "Holly. *Seriously*."

I sighed, exasperated. "Look, have you ever talked to her? I mean, *really* talked to her? She's, like, the most stuck-up person on the planet!"

Now Gabby looked totally mystified. "Really? We sit next to each other in computer lab. I thought she seemed pretty cool."

She couldn't be serious. For a moment, I was too

shocked to say anything. It was one thing that this girl had Julia fooled. They shared a cabin at band camp; they kind of *had* to become friends. But I thought it had to be pretty obvious to everyone else that Natasha was a mega-phony.

"Look how she is in band," I said when I finally found my voice. "She's such a know-it-all! Always talking about how easy everything is—she even said "Labyrinthine Dances" was easy, remember?"

Gabby shrugged. "I don't know; I guess I never noticed." She dragged the last cinnamon stick across her plate, scraping up all the frosting. "Holly—and don't take this the wrong way—but are you maybe just mad that she got first chair instead of you?"

I crossed my arms. "Well, technically I *did* play the chair test better." As soon as the words were out of my mouth, I cringed. Did that sound obnoxious? It was true, but still.

But Gabby just looked thoughtful. "You sounded great, definitely. But, I mean, so did Natasha."

Sighing, I glanced over at the booth where Mr. Dante was sitting. "But, Gabby, I played it *perfectly*. I'm not saying Natasha isn't good, but she didn't play it exactly right like I did. I don't . . . I don't understand why Mr. Dante gave her first chair."

Gabby set her plate down next to the stacks of cups. "Okay, so you played exactly what was on the page. But you know, it's not always about that."

I had no idea what she was talking about. It must

have showed on my face, because Gabby laughed.

"Look, you and Natasha both sounded awesome," she said. "And it's really not that big a deal, right? First chair, second chair, whatever."

Um, it was kind of a *huge* deal. First was better than second. Duh.

But I just smiled at her. "Yeah, right."

Aaron was standing over by the air hockey table on the opposite side of the room. I couldn't help but notice his shirt was the same color blue as my dress. We matched. It was a thought so dorky, I wasn't even sure I'd tell Julia if she were here. And if we were on speaking terms.

Aaron watched the game intently, high-fiving Brooke when she scored one on Liam Park. I could see the smile parentheses from here.

"Oh my God, just go *talk* to him already."

Gabby was grinning at me. I felt my cheeks burn.

"What?"

"Go talk to him," Gabby repeated, looking pointedly at Aaron. I shook my head.

"Why not?" she said. "He's really nice."

"I know he is," I said, trying to sound casual. "I've talked to him before."

"So go do it now."

I looked over at Aaron again, and my stomach started flip-flopping. I shook my head again, toying with my turtle necklace.

"Nope. Too nervous."

Gabby rolled her eyes. "Come on, Holly. He's just a guy." She pushed me, and I stumbled forward a few steps.

"Fine!" I tried to glare at her. "But if you see me standing over there drooling like a moron, you'd better come save me."

"Deal."

I had to navigate around the growing line at the buffet and the cluster of people waiting for their turn at Skee-Ball. By the time I got to the air hockey table, Brooke had apparently beaten Liam, because Gabe Fernandez had taken his place. Aaron was still standing by the table, but he wasn't paying attention to the game anymore.

Because he was talking to Natasha.

I stopped, staring at them. Why was she talking to Aaron? Why was she giggling at whatever he was saying? Why was she *touching his arm?*

Gabe scored a goal to scattered applause, and Aaron glanced back at the game. When he did, for the briefest of seconds, Natasha's eyes flickered in my direction.

And she smiled.

It happened so fast, I almost didn't catch it. Then realization dawned, and my stomach clenched.

Before rehearsal, in the cubby room. Julia had been teasing me about hanging around her locker. Natasha must have realized we were talking about Aaron. Either that, or she'd managed to get Julia to tell her that I . . . how I felt about him.

She was doing this on *purpose*.

I walked away from the table. My face felt like it was on fire. I leaned against the entrance to the arcade room, listening to the beeps and pings and yells and trying to think clearly.

But thinking clearly was hard at this level of apoplectic.

It wasn't enough that this girl was first chair. It wasn't enough that just two weeks at band camp had bumped her to best friend status with Julia. It wasn't enough that her grades were perfect and her hair was perfect and her dress and boots were almost exactly like mine.

She had to steal Aaron, too.

Not that Aaron was *mine*. But did Natasha even *like* him, really? Or was she just doing this to get revenge because of a little spit on her shoe? I mean, she'd never mentioned liking him before.

I pictured the way she'd glanced at me and smiled just now, and my hands clenched into fists at my sides.

Applause broke out again around the air-hockey table. Judging from the high fives, it looked like Brooke had beaten Gabe, too. Aaron said something to Natasha, then moved to the end of the table. I waited until he and Brooke started to play before walking over and tapping Natasha on the shoulder.

She turned, and her eyes widened. "Oh! Um . . . hi."

"Can I talk to you for a sec?" I kept my voice light, but Natasha glanced around nervously.

"Yeah, okay."

We left the table and walked over to a pinball machine no one was playing. I took a deep breath. Maybe I was angry, but I wasn't about to embarrass myself in front of everyone by crying or screaming or something equally stupid.

I crossed my arms tightly over my chest and faced Natasha.

"First of all, I'm sorry about today. With the spit valve. It was an accident."

"Okay." I could tell by her smirk that she didn't believe me. "Is that all?"

"No." Steeling myself, I took a deep breath. "Why were you talking to Aaron just now?"

Natasha shrugged. "Why not?"

"I just think it's kind of weird," I said slowly, "considering you've never mentioned him before. Did Julia tell you?"

"Tell me what?"

Stop playing dumb, I wanted to scream. But I kept my voice calm. "That I . . . you know. Did she tell you I like him?"

Natasha chewed her bottom lip. "Do you?"

I raised an eyebrow. "Do *you*? Or are you just flirting with him to make me mad?"

Her mouth fell open. I was kind of surprised I said it, too. But I kept my face neutral. After a second, Natasha closed her mouth. Then she smiled.

"Jeez, Holly." Her tone was different, suddenly. She

was talking to me like I was five years old, and it was making the thudding in my ears even louder. "You *really* don't like competition, do you?"

"Excuse me?"

"Be honest." Natasha examined her fingernails, which were the exact same shade of pink as her dress. "You've been acting a little weird since the whole chair-test thing. It really bothers you that I beat you, doesn't it."

It wasn't a question. I opened my mouth, but nothing came out.

"That's why you're always on my case in band," she continued, wearing an expression of mock sympathy. "Trying to suck up to Mr. Dante, pointing out every mistake I make."

"*Me?*" A few kids by the air-hockey table glanced over at us, and I lowered my voice. "*You're* the one who—"

"That's why you emptied your spit valve on my shoe." She shook her head sadly. "Come on, Holly. No way was that an accident. Everyone knows it."

I opened my mouth, but nothing came out.

"And now we're at a party," Natasha went on, "and all I do is talk to some guy, and you jump all over me!"

I could not believe this. She was twisting everything around, making it seem like this was all my fault. I mean, maybe she was right about the shoe thing. But *she* started all this. I finally found my voice.

"The only reason you're acting all interested in Aaron is—"

"What? Is he your boyfriend or something?" she interrupted, and I hated myself for blushing.

"No."

"Then I haven't done anything wrong."

"Really." I forced myself to speak slowly. "So you didn't do it just to try to make me jealous."

"Nope."

"So you're saying you like Aaron."

She paused. "Maybe I do."

We glared at one another. After a moment, I broke the silence.

"Tell me the truth. Did Julia tell you I like him?"

Natasha rolled her eyes. "What does Julia have to do with this?"

"Everything!" I exploded. "She's never told anyone any of my secrets, ever. So if she told you, you must have . . . tricked her, or something."

"*Tricked* her?" Natasha laughed. "You know, you're not the only friend Julia has. We tell each other everything, too."

"Please," I snapped. "So you spent two weeks at band camp together. Big deal. Julia's been my best friend since third grade and—"

I stopped, because suddenly all I could think about was what Julia would say if she could see Natasha and me fighting right now. Taking a deep breath, I started over.

"Look. Maybe we just need to—to call a truce, or something."

Natasha raised an eyebrow. "A truce?"

Another eruption of cheers from the air-hockey table caused us both to look over. A few kids were patting Brooke on the back, while the rest wandered off to other games. I turned back to Natasha.

"Yeah, a truce," I said. "Julia wouldn't want—"

"Hey!"

The words caught in my throat, because Aaron had materialized at my side. Between that and arguing with Natasha, my bones suddenly felt like rubber.

"Hi!" Natasha and I both said at the same time. Aaron smiled at both of us, and I noticed he was holding two air hockey mallets.

"You said you wanted to try a game, right?" he said to Natasha. "Brooke's done beating all of us now, so . . . want to play?"

Natasha looked at me for a second. Then she smiled.

"I'd love to."

Without another word to me, they headed to the table together.

My entire body felt numb. I stood there for about three seconds before a familiar burning started behind my eyes.

Nope. I was not crying at the band party, not with Natasha and Aaron and everyone else right there. Blinking furiously, I shoved my way past a few kids trying to play some race-car game. I was vaguely aware of someone calling my name, but all I cared about was getting to the door before the tears started—I didn't want to talk to Gabby or anyone else. I was almost there when a hand touched my arm.

"What?" I yelled, swiveling around. Owen took a step back, blinking so rapidly it was kind of alarming.

"Are you okay?"

"I'm fine," I snapped. "What do you want?"

He glanced behind him uncertainly. "We've got an *Alien Invaders* tournament going on," he said, and through the haze that was already starting in my eyes, I noticed Trevor and several others gathered around a game just inside of the arcade room. "It's a lot like *Prophets*, I thought maybe you'd—"

"Not right now, Owen." The tears were seconds from spilling over. I had to get outside. So when Owen started to say something else, I lost it.

"Look, I don't care about some stupid video game—just leave me alone!"

I turned quickly and pushed through the exit. But not before seeing the hurt expression on Owen's face.

When the door swung closed behind me, the silence was overwhelming. I walked half a block away from Spins before sinking down on the curb, pulling my knees into my chest, and crying.

All weekend, I replayed my argument with Natasha in my head. When I woke up Monday morning, I was still angry. I was still hurt. I was still embarrassed. But at least I'd decided on one thing.

Forget the whole truce idea.

Sitting next to Natasha in band was just about as intolerable as "Labyrinthine Dances," which Mr. Dante had still been rehearsing at a ridiculously slow tempo. After spending ten minutes on four tedious measures, we finally got to the second page. On the other side of Natasha, I heard Gabby groan softly.

"Saxes and clarinets," said Mr. Dante, flipping a page in his score, "this section is all about you. Take a minute to finger through the part—everyone else, let's hear measures eighty-four through ninety-five."

I sighed inwardly. The horns had four measures of rest before we were supposed to play, and I counted through them silently while Mr. Dante conducted. Next to me, Natasha lifted her horn a measure early and played a few notes before realizing her mistake. She stopped, and Mr. Dante cut the band off.

I couldn't see her, but I knew Natasha was just waiting for me to say something. I sat very, very still, staring at my lap. An ant crawled across my knee, and I flicked it off, wrinkling my nose.

"Four measures of rest, Natasha," said Mr. Dante, and she blushed. "Trombones, we missed a few accidentals in there—Trevor, make sure you're playing a C-sharp in measure eighty-six. Let's try it again."

I arranged my face into a neutral expression, even though inside I was doing a happy dance. Stupid, sure, but hey—I didn't have much to be happy about today.

Julia and I had made up over the phone on Sunday. Sort of. I called her, we both said we were sorry, and she said she was stressed about history, and I said I was stressed, too. But I hadn't told her about what happened at the band party.

Because I still hated Natasha, and Julia knew it, and she still liked Natasha, and I knew it. So our friendship wasn't the same anymore. And obviously I wasn't about to eat lunch with the two of them.

I didn't think I could eat with Owen, either—not after I yelled at him like that. It was bad enough that I would have to sit with him in science. I couldn't even look at him without remembering the expression on his face right before I'd run out of Spins.

So I told Julia I was practicing during lunch. And

it was only a half lie—after I ate in the bathroom, I was planning on going to the practice rooms. (I'd so rather just eat there, but I wasn't about to break Mr. Dante's no-food rule.)

After we plodded through "Labyrinthine Dances" for another ten minutes, Mr. Dante asked us to take out "Galactic March," one of the songs we were performing at the football game. "Thank God," I heard Trevor mumble behind me.

"This one's coming along nicely," Mr. Dante said after we played it all the way through once. "Actually, I think we might be able to perform it at the pep rally Thursday."

I slumped a little bit in my chair. The march had the horn solo, and I wanted to be the one playing it at the football game. But the chair test wasn't until next week, so it looked like Natasha would be playing it Thursday. In front of the whole school. That would really help her ego.

"Holly, I'll need you to play the solo at the pep rally."

I stared at Mr. Dante blankly. He hadn't just said that. He couldn't have read my mind.

But next to me, Natasha was sitting up rigidly, her eyes wide. "Um, I . . . why?" she sputtered. Mr. Dante waved a slip of paper at her.

"Because you won't be there," he said. "Thursday afternoon is the first debate meet, right? Ms. Monroe notified your teachers that you, Leah, and Liam would be absent."

"I thought we were supposed to be back by seventh

period." Natasha's voice was weirdly high.

Liam Park spoke up from the tuba section. "They changed the start time of the meet from one thirty to two, remember? Ms. Monroe told us yesterday."

Natasha looked devastated. I had to press my lips together tight to keep from smiling.

"Let's run through this one more time," Mr. Dante said. "Go ahead and give the solo a shot, Holly."

"Okay!"

My stomach was all fluttery, which made it hard to play. The whole solo was sixteen measures, but the first measure was nothing but French horn—the whole band stopped playing. (I'd already marked it with a blue highlighter.) Halfway through the march, I heard a weird, raspy noise coming from the saxes. I was relieved and disappointed when Mr. Dante waved for us to stop playing.

"Gabby, what's going on?"

"I don't know!" Gabby was fiddling with her mouthpiece. "Something's wrong, I can't figure it out."

Mr. Dante stepped off the podium. "Take your reed off," he said, walking over to the end of our row. Gabby tried, making a face.

"My ligature's stuck," she said. Mr. Dante raised his eyebrows.

"You do know you're supposed to clean your mouthpiece every day, Gabby," he said. "Don't you?"

I tried not to laugh as Gabby gave him an innocent look. "Maybe not *every* day."

"Ew," Natasha whispered, flicking an ant off her arm. Shifting in my chair, I peered at the floor and noticed another one making its way toward my sandals. Just as I kicked at it, Natasha shrieked.

"Oh my God!"

She leaped out of her chair and stumbled past me. Alarmed, I watched as Gabby half stood out of her chair, holding her mouthpiece far out in front of her. Tiny black specks scurried over her hand.

"Ants," she said calmly. "There are ants in my saxophone."

Chaos erupted. In front of Gabby, Sophie and two flute players screamed and ran to the front of the room; behind me, Trevor yelled, "Awesome!" and climbed over Natasha's chair to see. I hovered over my chair, torn between wanting to get a look and moving as far away from the ants as possible.

Mr. Dante took Gabby's sax and mouthpiece up to the podium and pulled out a spray bottle. "Back to your seats," he said mildly, removing the ligature and spraying the mouthpiece. Gabby stood next to him, wiping her arm with a rag.

"So this," he informed us, "is what happens when you don't clean your instrument. And especially when you eat sugary stuff right before you play." He gave Gabby a meaningful look before glancing up at the clock. "Go ahead and pack up for today. Gabby, go get your case and bring it over here. We're going to have a cleaning lesson."

In the cubby room, Natasha was still freaking out. "They were on my arm," she moaned, rubbing her elbow. I waited until she left before rolling my eyes.

"I wonder if Gabby actually *ate* any ants," Trevor was saying as he opened his case. "That would be so cool."

Owen and I both laughed, then glanced at each other. He looked away quickly, and I felt my face get hot. On the other side of the cubby room, Julia was giggling as Natasha showed off her nonexistent ant bites. She'd probably spend the whole lunch period talking about it.

It almost made eating by the toilets appealing.

When I got to the bathroom, I headed straight to the sinks to wash my hands. (Maybe I wasn't as squeamish as Natasha, but still. That *was* pretty gross.) The noise from the hand dryer covered up the sound of the door opening, so when I turned around and Gabby was right there, I had a small heart attack.

"You scared me!" I exclaimed, and she grinned.

"Sorry." Moving to the mirror, Gabby inspected her arm before pumping soap into her hand. "That was pretty cool, huh?"

I couldn't help but laugh. "Um, disgusting is more like it."

Gabby shrugged. "Well, don't worry. Mr. Dante said he's going to check every day to make sure I clean my sax." Rinsing her hands, she glanced at me. "So . . . you doing okay?"

"What do you mean?"

She rolled her eyes. "You know what I mean. You and Natasha."

In the mirror, I could see my face turning red. "Oh."

"Sophie heard you guys fighting at the party," Gabby said, leaning against the sinks. "She told Julia."

My head snapped up. "What? When?"

"Just now, after band." Gabby gave me a sympathetic look. "Her cubby's right next to Julia's. I tried to get her to shut up, but . . ."

She didn't finish, but I understood. Sophie Wheeler was a huge gossip.

"Did she . . . did she hear exactly what we were fighting about?" If everyone found out about the whole Aaron thing, I was transferring schools.

"Well, Julia." Gabby tilted her head, scrutinizing me. "That *is* what you were fighting about, right? Julia?"

"Yeah," I said quickly. "So what, um . . . what did Julia say?"

Gabby lifted a shoulder. "Nothing, really. But she looked pretty bummed."

Ugh. Leaning against the wall next to the hand dryers, I sank down to the floor. "Well, good thing I'm staying in here for lunch."

"You aren't going to talk to her?"

"Who, Julia? Not now—Natasha has our lunch."

Gabby looked surprised. "Actually, that's who I meant. Natasha."

I stared at her. "Why in the world would I want to talk to her?"

"Because you had a fight. Because she's Julia's friend. Because she's really not so bad, and maybe if you tried to—"

"But she *is*!" This was too much. "Maybe you and Julia and everybody else haven't figured it out yet, but you will sooner or later. And that fight was *so* not my fault—unless Natasha wants to apologize to me, I've got nothing to say to her."

It all came out a little harsher than I meant it to, but I couldn't help it. I just could not *believe* this girl had everyone fooled.

Taking a step back, Gabby picked up her backpack. "Okay. Anyway, I've got PE See you later." She slipped out the door without looking at me.

So somehow in the last three days, I'd managed to screw things up with Julia, Owen, *and* Gabby. At the rate things were going, the whole school would hate me by the end of the week.

Everything was totally messed up. And obviously it was all Natasha's fault.

Julia never said anything to me about my fight with Natasha at the band party. It should have been a relief, but it wasn't. I figured she just didn't want to hear me complain about Natasha again. Or maybe she just didn't care at all anymore. After all, Julia hadn't said anything about me not eating with them in the cafeteria all week. And somehow I didn't think she believed my lame excuse about practicing.

Only one thing made me feel a tiny bit better—Julia was kind of acting weird around Natasha, too. And Natasha had definitely noticed, because she'd been pretty subdued. Even better, I didn't have to see her at all on Thursday, thanks to the debate meet. But I couldn't even enjoy it because I was so nervous about the pep rally.

I'd practiced the solo for "Galactic March" every

single night this week while Chad banged on the wall and yelled at me to stop. I could play it frontward and backward. But literally the entire school would be at the pep rally. And the gym made everything so . . . *loud*.

I had to nail it, though. I wanted Mr. Dante to realize that I should've been first chair all along.

"You'll do fine," Julia said as she turned yet another cracker into dust. "You sounded great today in band."

"Thanks." My own lunch bag sat unopened on the table. I was so nervous, I couldn't even enjoy eating at an actual table again, instead of my usual bathroom stall. "It's just a little scary. I mean, this is our first real performance—it's a big deal!"

As soon as the words were out of my mouth, I wanted to hit myself. It *was* a big deal—and Julia couldn't be a part of it.

"Sorry," I started, but she waved me off.

"It's okay."

"You'll get to play at the football game, though," I said firmly. "I know it." I started to ask how history was going, but stopped at the dejected look on her face.

Apparently, it wasn't going well.

I felt even worse during computer lab seventh period when the vice-principal's voice crackled over the intercom, asking teachers to release the football players, cheerleaders, and band members to get ready for the pep rally. Julia wished me luck, and I had to leave her there doing our stupid spreadsheet activity.

By the time I pushed the doors open to the band

hall, my stomach was doing massive flip-flops. Everyone chatted noisily as they put their instruments together, but I stayed silent. Vomiting was totally a possibility if I opened my mouth.

Besides, there wasn't anyone to talk to. Julia was stuck in class. Gabby didn't seem mad, but she wasn't exactly going out of her way to talk to me (not that I could blame her).

And Owen . . . yeah, that was still all messed up too. On Monday in science, I'd waited until Mrs. Driscoll had us start our labs. Then as soon as I sat down at our workstation, I'd started to apologize.

"I'm sorry I yelled at you at the party. I was . . ." And then I'd stopped, because really, I had no idea what else to say. I didn't want to tell him about Natasha, and there was no *way* I'd ever tell him about Aaron.

So I just sat there like an idiot with my mouth open until he'd said: "It's okay."

But all week, we just did our labs and barely talked about anything but science stuff. I hadn't even asked about studying together again. Our video game hangs were probably over.

The thought made me sad.

When I got to the gym, Mr. Dante was organizing us into rows up the bleachers. By the time we finished warming up, students were filing in, and my stomach started a new bout of flipping. (Seeing Aaron in his football jersey so did not help that one bit.)

The pep rally started, and we played the fight

song while the cheerleaders did their routine. Then the coaches started talking while my fingers tapped away nervously on my horn. Squinting at the bleachers opposite us, I spotted Julia.

All of a sudden, I missed her so much it hurt. I missed her more than I had when she was at Lake Lindon. Like she was across the state right now, instead of across the gym.

Next to me, Gabby was twisted all the way around, talking to Victoria. I glanced on the other side of Brooke and saw Owen facing the row behind us, too. He, Trevor, and another trombone player all had their heads lowered. Leaning back slightly, I noticed the Warlock cards spread out over the bleachers and smiled to myself.

Just for a second, though.

"All right, folks—'Galactic March'!" Mr. Dante stood up in front of us, and my heart leaped into my throat. *Not yet, I'm not ready!* I wanted to scream, but instead I opened my flip folder to the march and took a deep breath.

I tried to focus, vaguely aware of Aaron hurrying up the bleachers and taking his seat with the trumpets behind me. Mr. Dante lifted his hands, I lifted my horn, and the song began.

Halfway through, my fingers were actually shaking, which made pressing down valves a lot harder than it should've been. The whole march seemed to fly by, and when we finally got to the solo, the heartbeat in my ears was louder than the whole percussion section.

I just had to get through that first measure—the part where the whole band stopped. If I could nail that, I'd be okay.

But I breathed in too much and too early. And my lips felt numb. And even though my brain said to press down two valves, I pressed three.

So when the band paused, the sound that came out of my horn was pretty much exactly how my brother described it.

A constipated moose.

Mr. Dante continued conducting as if nothing had happened, and the low brass and percussion came in right on time. But there was no horn solo, because I was frozen. A statue of the world's worst French horn player, sitting right there on the bleachers in the Millican Middle School gym.

A few of the clarinet players glanced back at me, and I heard laughter over the music. Mr. Dante was looking at me as he conducted. He didn't look angry, just quizzical. *Are you going to play, Holly?*

Somehow I managed to inhale, move my fingers, and play. But I was so freaked by what had just happened that my tone was weak and shaky, and I missed three notes.

It was literally the worst performance ever. Not just *my* worst performance. The worst performance in all of music history. It had to be.

When "Galactic March" ended, I put my horn in my

lap and stared at it, waiting for the entire band to crack up. A few of the flute players were looking at me and giggling, and out of the corner of my eye I saw Gabby watching me. But other than that, everyone was just back to talking.

As far as I could see, anyway. I so wasn't about to turn around. If Aaron was laughing at me, I didn't want to know.

Even though it was no more than ten minutes, the rest of the pep rally seemed to drag on forever. As soon as Mr. Dante dismissed us, I flew down the steps without looking around and practically ran out of the gym.

I beat everyone back to the band hall, packed up my horn, grabbed my backpack, and hurried back into the halls just as the bell rang. When I spotted Gabby and a few others from band coming down the corridor, I ducked out the closest exit.

I leaned against the brick wall, trying to make myself invisible as students swarmed out of the building and toward the buses lining the curb. My face was hot with humiliation. Tears pricked at my eyes, but I blinked them away.

Normally after something this traumatic, I'd go over to Julia's and she'd make me laugh so much I'd forget about whatever happened. But I couldn't do that, because Natasha might be there. I knew she'd hear the whole story eventually, but there was no way I could deal with her smug face right now.

Besides, things were so weird with Julia, I wasn't even sure if I wanted to confide in her right now.

Squeezing my eyes shut, I took a deep breath. I needed someone to talk to, and something fun to take my mind off the fact that I'd just made a complete idiot of myself in front of the entire school.

I needed a friend. And maybe a few aliens to blow up.

I watched as my bus pulled away from the curb. Then I picked up my case and my bag and started walking.

When I knocked on Owen's door, a tall, broad-shouldered man answered.

"Can I help you?" he asked. A little girl with reddish hair and purple paint smudged on her face peered at me from behind his legs.

"Uh . . ." I wasn't sure what to say—who were these people? Glancing around, I wondered if I'd knocked at the wrong house. "Is, um . . . is Owen here?"

He smiled. "He sure is. And you are?"

"That's Holly, Steve!"

I breathed a sigh of relief when Mrs. Grady appeared. "One of Owen's friends from school. Come in!"

"Thanks." I stepped into the foyer and set my horn case by the door.

"That looks like Owen's," said the little girl, and I nodded.

"Yup, we both play French horn."

"Holly, this is Owen's stepsister, Megan," said Mrs. Grady. "And this is my husband, Steve."

"Nice to meet you, Mr. Grady." I shook his hand just as Worf bounded down the stairs. "Hi, Worf!"

"Owen's in the game room," Steve said. "Come on up."

I followed him upstairs, Megan and Worf in tow. Owen was so focused on whatever he was doing on the computer that he didn't notice us.

"Owen, you've got company," Mr. Grady said, picking up a basketball on the floor next to the couch.

Owen swiveled in his chair. "Oh! Um . . . hi, Holly." That was followed by about a million blinks.

"Hi," I said nervously.

"Hi," said Megan, and I couldn't help but giggle.

"All right, Megs. Let's go finish up with finger painting." Mr. Grady turned back to the stairs, still holding the basketball. "Hey, Owen—want to shoot a few hoops after dinner?"

"Uh . . ." Owen glanced back at his computer. "Sure, maybe. If I finish this."

I leaned on the couch's armrest and waited until Mr. Grady and Megan were downstairs and out of earshot. "So . . . you like basketball?"

Owen sat back down in his chair, watching Worf attack his shoelaces. "It's okay." He paused. "Actually, no. I hate it. But Steve really wants me to play."

"Oh," I said. "He and Megan answered the door. I thought I was at the wrong house for a minute."

"Steve usually works till seven, but he got off early today," Owen replied. "Megan lives with her mom half the time."

"Oh."

Cue the awkward silence. *Just apologize,* my brain yelled, and I swallowed.

"I had this big fight with Natasha at the band party and I know this sounds stupid but she made me so mad I just had to leave and I didn't want to cry in front of everybody and that's why I yelled at you but I didn't mean to and I didn't mean what I said and I'm really really *really* sorry."

It all spilled out in one breath. If I wasn't so nervous, I'd laugh at the expression on Owen's face. He kind of looked terrified. But really, I *had* sounded pretty psychotic.

"Okay." Blinkblinkblink.

"I mean it," I said emphatically. "And today was pretty much awful, too, and if it's okay with you I'd really like to play *Prophets*. Please."

Owen stared at me for another second, then laughed. "Okay."

Relieved, I flopped down on the couch as he grabbed the controllers off the floor. "So tell me the truth. Was everyone making fun of me after the pep rally?"

"What?" Owen paused with the remote aimed at the TV. "No, why?"

"You know why!" I exclaimed. "'Galactic March'! The solo, I totally screwed it up."

"Oh, that." Owen shrugged. "No, I didn't hear anyone say anything."

"Seriously?" I wondered if he was just being nice. Again. "But it was so awful!"

"It wasn't *that* bad."

"Owen." I gave him a stern look. "I sounded like a constipated moose."

He burst out laughing, and after a few seconds I was grinning, too.

"Okay, so you messed up," he said after a minute. "But I bet it wasn't as bad as you think it was."

I snorted. "If you say so."

But I felt a little better. And after forty-five minutes of total alien carnage, I felt a *lot* better. When Trevor showed up, I jumped up off the couch.

"You always leave when I get here," Trevor said, grabbing my controller. "Look, I won't say anything about how bad you are at this. Even though you're bad. Really, *really* bad."

I glared at him. "Put my controller down—I'm not leaving. I was just going to call my mom and ask her to pick me up at five thirty."

I raced down to the kitchen, made the call, and raced back up to the game room.

Ten minutes later, I'd killed sixteen aliens and blown up three pods. "Wow, Trevor," I said, not taking my eyes off the screen. "You've only killed twelve, huh? Better catch up." Trevor grumbled something I couldn't understand.

By five twenty-five, I was really glad he didn't have a drink to "accidentally" spill in my lap. Especially when I hijacked his tank and used it to blow up my sixth pod.

"What—why did you—" he sputtered, throwing down his controller and glaring at me. Owen was lying on his side, laughing. I gave Worf a last pat on the head, then stood.

"Sorry, Trevor. Guess you just need a little more practice." Smiling brightly, I picked up my backpack. "Bye, Owen!"

"Bye, Holly." He was still laughing.

Halfway down the stairs, I heard Trevor mumble, "Dude, I wish you'd quit inviting her over." I smiled to myself.

What a sore loser.

Chapter Eighteen

One friendship fixed, two more to go.

Before school on Monday, I stopped by the vending machines. When I got to English, I tossed a bag of M&M's on Gabby's desk. She glanced up in surprise.

"Sorry I was such a jerk last week," I said. "I thought about what you said, and you're right."

Gabby blinked. "You mean about Natasha?"

"Yup." I sat down at my desk. "She's Julia's friend, and I need to just . . . deal with it." *Until Julia realizes she's evil*, I added in my head.

"Cool." Gabby ripped open the bag, and I accepted a handful of M&M's. "She's really pretty nice, Holly. I think you'll like her once you get to know her."

I put on my biggest smile. "I bet you're right."

Not.

But until she and Julia and everyone else realized how awful Natasha was, I was going to fake it. I'd be so over-the-top nice, I'd out-fake Natasha herself (if that was even humanly possible). I'd be nice even when she started going on and on about herself. Even when she flirted with Aaron during band because he sat behind us and she knew it bothered me. Even when she droned on and on about debate team during lunch (and anyway, eating in the girls bathroom was getting seriously old).

If Natasha and I at least fake–getting along would make Julia happy, then that's what I'd try to do. Because I was Julia's best friend, and I wasn't giving up that title without a fight.

For the rest of the week, I stuck with the plan. Julia's history test was next Wednesday, and she had to pass if she was going to play at the football game. Lunch every day pretty much consisted of her crumbling cookies all over her notes without ever eating a bite, Natasha drilling her endlessly with those stupid flash cards, and me trying to sit at an angle so I could stare at Aaron across the cafeteria without being totally obvious.

"Holly?"

I glanced at Julia, blinking, and she laughed.

"I said your name, like, four times. What are you staring at?"

Hastily, I pointed at the front of the lunch line. (I was *not* in the mood to discuss Aaron in front of Natasha.)

"Seth is over there," I said, giving Julia a pointed look. "If he comes over to say hi again, try to remember his name." I paused for emphasis. "It's *Seth*."

Julia kicked me under the table, laughing. "For your information, we had an actual conversation in PE yesterday." She pulled out another handful of crackers before adding, "It was about how bad the weight room smells. But still."

The three of us spent pretty much the rest of lunch talking about Seth Anderson, the gym, and how it was kind of gross that the winter dance was in the stinkiest room in the entire school. Everything felt normal, almost. Until Natasha started talking about what to wear to the dance.

"I'll definitely need to go shopping in a few weeks," she said. "Get something new, you know?"

"I've already got something new—that red dress," Julia replied, popping a cracker into her mouth. "I mean, I didn't get to wear it to the band party."

At the words "band party," I flinched. None of us looked at one another.

"Right. You should totally wear that," Natasha said at last. I nodded mutely, and Julia went back to destroying her crackers.

I couldn't wait to get to science. Band and lunch were so awkward every day, it was quickly becoming my favorite class.

How pathetic.

Owen had already made a new batch of cards for the chapter we started this week. And hey, at least I wasn't totally lost anymore. In fact, the labs were actually starting to make sense.

At the end of class on Thursday, Mrs. Driscoll gave us all a sheet to take home.

"'Fifteenth Annual Oak Point School District Science Fair,'" I read, making a face. "Yuck."

"Please give this to your parents and mark it on your calendars," Mrs. Driscoll announced. "The fair isn't until May, but participation is mandatory. You and your lab partner will begin working on your project at the start of next semester. Yes, for a grade," she added when Trevor raised his hand. "We'll discuss this more before winter break."

"How fun," I muttered.

"I know!" Owen exclaimed. I glanced at him and bit my lip to keep from laughing, because he obviously meant it. "Hey, are you coming over today?"

"I can't," I replied. "I'm staying after school to practice for the chair test next week without Chad pounding on my wall."

Owen smiled. "You really want to beat Natasha, huh?"

"No." Apparently I said it too quickly, because he laughed. "Okay, yeah, I do. But not just because of Natasha. I want another shot at the horn solo. After the whole pep rally thing, I need to redeem myself."

And I meant it, too. Yes, seeing my name above Natasha's would be pretty sweet. Okay, *very* sweet. But I was irritated with myself for screwing up so badly last Friday. When I got to the band hall after school, I made sure Mr. Dante saw me through his office window before heading into a practice room. He waved at me from his desk.

I started with a quick warm-up, then took out the chorale. It was weird—the chorale really was pretty easy, but . . .

I didn't sound bad, and I was playing it right. But it didn't sound *great*.

After half an hour, I got up and knocked on Mr. Dante's open door. He glanced up from his computer.

"Hi, Holly," he said. "What's up?"

"Would you listen to me play the chorale?" I asked. "I need help."

"Of course!"

He followed me back to the practice room. I sat down, picked up my horn, and waited for whoever was playing in the room next to me to stop so I could concentrate.

Mr. Dante leaned against the wall and bowed his head, but I could tell he was listening closely. When I finished, I frowned.

"You don't look too happy," Mr. Dante said.

"Well, it's just that I played it right," I said. "But it sounds . . . blah."

He laughed. "Blah?"

"I mean, it just . . ." I shrugged. "It's boring."

"Okay." Mr. Dante tilted his head. "So is it the music that's boring?"

"Maybe," I said with a grin, and he laughed again. "No, it's me. I can't make it sound good."

I tried not to show how much this bothered me. I knew the chorale wasn't boring, because we played it in class and I sat next to Natasha.

And I would never say this to anyone, but she made it sound *amazing*.

"So what do you think you're doing wrong?" Mr. Dante asked. I studied the music, frowning again.

"I don't know. I didn't miss any notes, I played all the rhythms right, I did all the dynamics, I—"

"What you're saying," Mr. Dante interrupted, "is that technically, you played it perfectly."

I blushed. "Well . . . yeah."

"You're right." He smiled. "You *did* play it perfectly. But music is about more than just playing something perfectly, right?"

"That's what Gabby said!" I exclaimed. "But I just . . . I don't really understand. What do you mean?"

Mr. Dante leaned forward and tapped the sheet of paper on my stand. "What's this?"

"Uh . . . my music?"

"This piece of paper is music?"

"Oh," I said. "No . . . it's paper with music written on it."

"Right," he said. "It's kind of a road map. Tells you what notes to play, how loud or soft to play them, what tempo—all that stuff. Will it sound exactly the same way with every musician, even if they do all that right?"

I drummed my fingers on my horn. "Probably not?"

He smiled. "Probably not. It's up to the musician

to actually make *music* out of it. You said you talked to Gabby about this—what do you think about her playing?"

"She's *amazing*," I said without hesitation.

"Why? Because she plays it perfectly?"

I kind of saw where he was going with this. "Well . . . no. I mean, she doesn't make any mistakes or anything, but that's not why she sounds so good."

"So what's the difference between how she sounds, and how you think you sound?"

I concentrated, remembering what Gabby sounded like on our first chair test. The music had been so easy, but it didn't sound boring at all when she played it.

"I don't know!" I sat back in my chair, frustrated. "I know it sounds different, but I don't know why."

"Sure you do," Mr. Dante said. "Music isn't notes on paper, right? It's a way of expressing ideas and emotions. You like listening to Gabby play because when she does, she's *saying* something."

I stared at him. I so badly wanted to understand, and when I thought about Gabby, I kind of did, but . . .

"I don't know how to do that. 'Say something,' or whatever."

"Then that," Mr. Dante said with a smile, "is something we're going to have to work on this year."

After he left, I gazed at the chorale for a little while, thinking. The person in the practice room next to me was working on it now, and they sounded great. Sitting up straight, I listened more closely.

Yup, that was definitely a trumpet.

Stomach tingling, I packed up my horn and folder and walked into the hall. When I paused outside of the next door and peered through the little window, the tingles turned to major flip-flops.

Apparently my hand had a mind of its own, because it knocked without my permission. Aaron glanced up, and I opened the door, embarrassed. He smiled at me.

"Hey, Holly!"

"Hi!" *Oh my God*. I didn't know what to say. Why had I knocked?

Luckily, Aaron spoke before the silence got awkward. "Was that you practicing next door? You sounded really good."

"Thanks!" I said, trying not to look like I wanted to turn cartwheels down the hall. "I guess I need the practice after how bad I screwed up at the pep rally."

Aaron laughed. "You mean the solo in the march?"

I felt my face get warm, even though he hadn't said it meanly. "Yeah. It was awful."

He shook his head. "Don't worry about it. Last year at the first football game, my first valve got stuck before we played the fight song, and I didn't notice. You know how the fight song starts, right?"

I nodded. (It started with a trumpet fanfare.)

Aaron pressed the valve and twisted it a little so it stayed halfway down. Then he lifted the trumpet to his mouth. "So we start the fight song, and this happens."

When he played, the most ridiculous noise I'd ever heard came out of his trumpet. I knew exactly what Chad would say it sounded like, but I wasn't going to say that because it was gross.

I did double over laughing in the doorway, though. Aaron grinned.

"Yeah, that's pretty much what everyone did," he said. "Mrs. Wendell had to start the song over again because half the trumpets were laughing instead of playing."

"Sorry," I managed to say, but I couldn't stop giggling.

He shrugged. "It's all right. I laughed, too. It *was* pretty funny."

"Yeah, it must have been."

"Anyway, it was way worse than the pep-rally thing," he said. "I promise."

"Thanks," I said. "That makes me feel better."

It made me feel a *lot* better, apparently. Because I couldn't stop smiling for the rest of the day.

Chapter Nineteen

"Are you *seriously* studying on a Saturday *again*?"

"Chad!" I yelled, glaring at him. "Can you *seriously* just please knock before you barge into my room?"

Rolling his eyes, Chad stepped back into the hall and shut my door. A second later:

Thud. Thud. Thud.

What a baby.

"Oh, just come in." Rolling my eyes, I turned my attention back to the cards scattered over my desk.

"I just downloaded *Deep Cove*," Chad said. "Wanna watch?"

I chewed my lip, shifting the cards around. "Maybe later, if that's okay. I need to finish this."

"You're kidding, right?" He picked up one of the cards and snorted. "What is all this?"

I grabbed the card out of his hand. "If you must know, I'm making these to help Julia. She's failing history."

"What's with all the dorky pictures?"

Sighing, I separated the cards into two groups. "These are my friend Owen's," I said, patting them. "He made this game in sixth grade to study history. I'm trying to make a game like it for Julia, only for seventh-grade history, obviously."

Chad stared at me dumbly. "A game?"

"Yeah." I stacked up Owen's cards and made two piles. "It's pretty cool, actually. See, this stack is all important people and events and stuff like that, and that stack is dates and places. Each player gets an even mix of cards from both stacks. So say you and I were playing, and I put down this card with Stephen F. Austin. You could win the hand if you had—"

"Oh my God, Holly." Chad was doing the squinty thing again, like it hurt to use his brain that much. "No offense, but your boyfriend sounds like a nerd."

"He's not a nerd," I said, standing up. "And he's my friend, not my boyfriend. Now get out so I can finish." I pushed Chad into the hallway and shut the door.

"What about *Deep Cove?*" he yelled.

"After dinner, maybe!" I yelled back, then sat down at my desk.

I was almost done making cards for all the people and events in the first three chapters of my history book. They didn't look nearly as good as Owen's, though. He had pictures on the back of each one of his, just like my science cards. And not like pictures he copied out of his textbook—original drawings. But these were even better than the ones he doodled during class. They were colored with ink so well, they almost looked like he'd printed them off his computer. One of the queens kind of looked like that troll from his napkin at lunch. Napoleon resembled one of the dwarves from *Snow White*.

It took forever to finish, but when I knocked on Julia's door Sunday afternoon I had all the cards we'd need to play the game in a plastic bag. (I'd done my best with the pictures, but most of them were pretty lame.)

"Hey!" Julia stepped back to let me in, eyeing the bag. "What's that?"

"This," I said confidently, "is what's going to help you pass your history test Wednesday."

An hour later, we were sitting on her bed studying our cards. We each had six left, plus two piles of the ones we'd already played. My pile was bigger, but Julia was improving fast.

"Battle of Velasco," I said, tossing the card down. "So you can put a date or a place."

Julia frowned at her cards. "Um . . ."

"Look." I flipped the card over and read off the back. "'This was the first battle between Mexico and Texas, and the—'"

"Got it!" Beaming, Julia put a card on top of mine.

"'June 1832,'" I read. "That's right!"

Julia collected both cards. "Hey, we're almost tied now!"

"Yup." I grinned at her. "See? You're getting it!"

"I know, I can't believe it." Julia shook her head. "Seriously, thanks for doing this, Holly."

"Anytime," I said. "Are you still going to tutoring?"

"Yeah, Dad takes me to school early every morning. My parents were seriously not happy about that progress report." Lowering her cards, Julia sighed. "And Natasha's been trying to help, too. But . . ."

I tried not to smirk. "It's not working?"

Julia shrugged. "She just . . . I don't know. History is pretty easy for her. That's why I didn't tell her when I failed the first few quizzes. I was embarrassed."

I blinked. "You mean Natasha didn't know you were failing until progress reports came out?"

"Yeah."

I pretended to study a card so Julia couldn't see how pleased I was. "Oh."

Julia snorted. "You don't have to look so happy about it."

Shaking my head frantically, I gave her my most innocent look. "I'm not!"

"Right." Julia turned the Battle of Velasco card over and over in her hands. "You know, Holly . . ." She stopped. "Never mind."

"What?"

She hesitated, then sat up straight. "Okay. Do you remember last year in English, when we had to memorize those poems and recite them in front of the class?"

"Yeah . . ."

"I was so *nervous*," Julia said. "I seriously almost puked in the bathroom that morning."

I stared at her. "Really? You never told me that."

"Right—because remember how excited you were about it?" She grinned at me. "You got *so* into it."

My cheeks felt warm. "I wasn't *that* excited."

"Holly, you wore a costume!"

"It was just a hat," I said defensively.

"You had props!"

"What, Chad's old stuffed monkey?" I exclaimed. "The poem was about the jungle! I just thought it would—" I stopped, because she was laughing. "Okay, what's your point?"

"My point is, I didn't tell you how nervous I was because you thought the whole thing was not only easy, but *cool*." Julia smiled. "I'm saying . . . yeah, Natasha is kind of a know-it-all. But so are you."

"Excuse me?" That stung, but I kept my tone light. "I am not!"

"Holly, I love you," Julia said, still grinning. "But yeah, you are."

"Okay, fine." I put my cards down. "But I'm nowhere near as bad as Natasha."

Julia's smile faded. "You really hate her, huh."

I played with my card, not meeting her gaze. I didn't want to say yes . . . but I didn't want to lie to Julia anymore, either.

"Look, Sophie told me you guys had a big fight at

the band party," Julia said at last.

Oh boy.

"Yeah, we did," I said slowly. "And I—I don't know what Natasha told you, but I didn't—"

"She didn't tell me anything," Julia interrupted. "Sophie said she heard you say something about me telling Natasha a secret about you, and then Natasha said you weren't my only friend. Or something like that. But Natasha never mentioned anything about it to me, and I never asked."

I drummed my fingers on my knee, unsure of what to say. But Julia spoke again before I got the chance.

"I don't know what you guys were arguing about," she said. "But Holly, of *course* I've never told Natasha a secret about you. Do you really think I'd do that?"

I winced. "No, I guess I don't. But . . ." I chewed my lip, and Julia stared at me.

"What?"

Ugh, I so did not want to say this. But I had to.

"I guess I just feel like maybe . . . maybe she's your best friend now."

Julia's eyes widened. "What? Why?"

I took a deep breath.

"Because you spent the last day of summer break with her and didn't even call me. Because you told her about your first kiss before me. Because you barely know this girl and it just seems like you'd rather hang out with her than you would with me."

After a few seconds, I forced myself to look at Julia.

Her mouth was hanging open.

"Holly," she said after a second. "I'm really sorry, I didn't know . . ." She paused, shaking her head. "Look. The day before school started, my dad dragged me all over the place shopping for school supplies. When we got home, Natasha called me, freaking out because they screwed up her schedule. I only asked her to come over because I think she was kind of nervous about starting at a new school."

"It's okay," I said hastily, already feeling guilty for bringing it up. "I—"

"No, listen." Julia sat up straighter. "The whole Garrett thing. Come on, Holly—I was *dying* to tell you about him! But we barely got any phone time while I was at the beach. And I mean, Natasha and I lived in the same cabin at Lake Lindon. I told her because . . . I don't know, I just had to tell *somebody*, you know?

"But, Holly," she went on before I could say anything. "You really think that means she's suddenly my best friend? That's just . . . there's no way. I promise."

I swallowed hard, my eyes burning. "Thanks," I whispered. Leaning across the bed, Julia hugged me.

"I have to ask you something, though," she said, flopping back against her pillows. "Why don't you like her, really? You didn't, right from the very beginning. Before you found out about Garrett and all that. How come?"

"She just . . . she's really stuck-up." It wasn't the first time I'd said that, but for some reason now it sounded lame. "I mean, it's like you said about history," I added quickly. "You didn't want to ask her for help because you were embarrassed—well, that's *her* fault. And it's not the same as the poem thing in English last year—I thought that was fun, but I wasn't *bragging* about it! Natasha's always talking about how easy history is, how easy *all* her classes are, how she's like the queen of debate team, or whatever. She thinks she's so good at everything. Doesn't it annoy you?"

Julia bit her lip like she was trying not to laugh. "No. I meant what I said—she reminds me of you."

I scowled. "Julia, I am *not* like her."

"No?" Julia started ticking off points on her fingers. "You both play French horn, and you're both awesome at it. You're both total perfectionists. Seriously, you're the only people I know who plan out what you're going to wear for an entire *week*, Holly. You even kind of have the same taste in clothes. You both—"

"But I don't *act* like her!" I cried. "I don't go around telling everyone how great I think I am."

"You don't?" Julia said. "What about this whole first chair thing? It's not just that you want it—it's that you think it's *wrong* that you didn't get it. Don't you?"

I opened my mouth to say no, but then I remembered standing near the buffet at Spins, talking to Gabby about the chair test.

I don't understand why Mr. Dante gave her first chair.

"Why are you so upset about second chair?" Julia asked. "I mean, jeez! We're already in advanced band with a bunch of eighth-graders. *And* you beat the only eighth-grader in your section! You're really good, Holly, and everyone knows it. So why is getting first chair such a big deal?"

"Because, it's . . ." I stopped, staring at the cards spread out on the bed. "I don't know."

"Because you're a perfectionist," Julia said again. "And so is Natasha. Nothing wrong with that! And why do you think I got along with her so well at band camp, anyway? She reminded me of my best friend. Who I really, really missed."

I didn't know what to say to that. Actually, I didn't want to say anything at all because there was a pretty good chance I'd cry.

Not because Julia had hurt my feelings—but because she was right.

"Look, maybe Natasha did act kind of . . . pushy at first," Julia admitted. "But, I mean, she just moved and had to start a new school. I was the only person she knew. She was just nervous. You know?"

I thought about Natasha's face when Julia and I had made that big scene in the hall on the first day of school. Then I imagined what I'd feel like if I'd started seventh grade someplace new. Someplace away from Julia and all my friends.

"Yeah," I said, and I was surprised to realize I actually meant it. "I know."

By the time I left Julia's house, she'd almost beaten me at the history game twice. Since she and her parents were going to visit her aunt on Sunday night, I watched *Deep Cove* with Chad. We'd just gotten to the creepiest part where this guy goes down to the basement of the theater where he works and this giant marionette from the show is down there and it starts moving even though there's no one controlling it and the guy starts to run but he trips and gets tangled up in all the string that's connected to the marionette and it's getting closer and closer and opening its mouth really, *really* wide, when the doorbell rang.

"Chad, I think your friends are here!" Mom called from the kitchen.

Groaning, I muted the computer. "Toby and Leon?"

"Yeah." Chad stood up and stretched. "We're ordering pizza, if you want some."

"Thanks," I said, getting up. "Let me know when it's here. I'll be in my room practicing."

"Oh, come *on*," Chad moaned. "Why do you have to—"

"Because I have another chair test Tuesday," I interrupted. "What's the big deal? Just hang out downstairs."

"You know Dad's watching the news." Chad glared at me. "Just, like, practice quiet or something, okay? Leon's bringing another movie."

"I can't just practice 'quiet.' It doesn't work that way," I informed him. "And what movie?"

"Don't know." Chad squinted. "I think he said it's something about ninjas and robots. Sounded kind of stupid, actually."

I blinked. "You mean *Cyborgs versus Ninjas*?"

Chad looked surprised. "Yeah, that's it. Have you seen it?"

"No, not yet," I said with a grin. "Let me know what you think, though."

I heard footsteps on the stairs and hurried to my room before Toby and Leon appeared. They weren't mean or anything, but when the three of them got together it was like they all lost whatever IQ points they had left. A girl could only take so much trollishness.

But I took my horn and music and went downstairs. Not because I was worried about annoying Chad—actually, I'd prefer to—but because I could hear the movie through the wall and I didn't want to cheat on my deal with Owen.

"Hey, Mom?"

Mom glanced up from her laptop. "Yes? Oh, hang on!" she exclaimed before I could speak. Shuffling through a stack of papers on the kitchen table, she pulled out a yellow envelope and handed it to me. "This came in the mail for you yesterday. I completely forgot."

"Ooh!" Setting my horn on the table, I turned it over eagerly. When I saw the name on the return address, my mouth dropped.

Natasha Prynne

"I'm assuming this is the Natasha you were telling me about, right?" Mom was watching me carefully.

"Yeah." I ripped the envelope open, pulled out the card, and stared at it in disbelief.

"What is it?"

"It's, um . . ." I flipped the card over, then read it a third time just to be sure I wasn't hallucinating. "She's having a birthday party next Saturday."

"Interesting. And you're invited?"

"I guess . . . yeah."

Mom looked like she was trying not to smile. "Interesting."

I glared at her. "You already said that."

She laughed. "So, are you going to go?"

Shrugging, I tossed the invitation onto the table. "Maybe. Anyway, can I practice in your and Dad's room?"

"Sure." Mom glanced at the ceiling. "More of those stupid horror movies?"

"They aren't stupid," I said defensively. "And no, they're watching one about robots and ninjas. Which *is* stupid."

"And possessed dolls aren't?"

I rolled my eyes. "Mom. They're *marionettes.*" She raised an eyebrow, and I shook my head, turning to leave the kitchen. "Whatever, you don't get it."

I heard her snort as she started typing again. "Got that right."

𝄞

Before school Monday, I dropped my horn off in the band hall and checked Julia's cubby. Her clarinet case was there—she must have come in early for tutoring. I wondered how pathetic it would be to go wait by her locker on the off-chance I'd see Aaron. Quite pathetic, I decided. But of course I was going to do it anyway.

Outside of the band hall, I ducked into the girls' room to check my hair. Ponytail or no ponytail? I was staring in the mirror, ready to pull out the elastic band, when I heard sniffling coming from one of the stalls.

Someone was crying.

I turned around and hesitated, wondering if I should say anything. Glancing down, I saw a pair of mint-green sandals with lots of straps laced around the ankles.

Someone with *really* cute shoes was crying. Clearly I had to do something.

I knocked lightly on the stall door. "Hey, are you okay?"

A few seconds of extra-hard sniffles passed before I heard a wobbly "Yeah."

"Okay." I waited a few seconds, then started to walk away.

"Oh, darn it!"

I stopped. "What's wrong?"

"Nothing, just . . . I'm out of tissue."

"Got it." I grabbed a bunch of paper towels and turned just as the stall door swung open and the girl stepped out.

Natasha.

We both froze, me still holding the towels out. Natasha's eyes were red and puffy, and her arms were crossed tightly over her chest. I opened my mouth, then closed it.

Five of the most awkward seconds in the history of the world passed.

"Um . . . thanks." With her other arm covering her shirt, Natasha stuck one hand out, and I remembered the towels.

"Oh! Yeah, you're welcome." I stood there uncertainly as she wiped her eyes. Her fingers were smudged with something black. "So, uh . . . what's wrong?"

Swallowing, Natasha glanced at me. "Nothing. I'm okay."

I immediately felt stupid for asking—why would she tell me? We weren't friends, even if she had invited me to her party. She'd probably just done that so Julia wouldn't be upset, anyway. I turned to leave, then remembered what Julia had said.

Why do you think I got along with her so well at band camp, anyway? She reminded me of my best friend.

Ugh.

Sighing, I faced Natasha again.

"Are you sure? You don't seem okay."

She stared at me, then let out a shaky laugh. "Okay, this is really stupid, but . . ." Natasha dropped both of her arms to her sides. Her white top was damp and smeared with black—it was totally ruined. I cringed.

"What happened?"

"I was doing my homework on the bus and my pen just exploded all over my shirt," she explained, wiping at it with the paper towel. "I came in here and tried to get it out, but the water only made it worse." Smiling tightly, Natasha looked up at me. "I know crying over a shirt must sound pretty stupid, but I've just had a really bad morning."

"It's not stupid," I reassured her. "On the first day of school my brother spilled orange juice all over my shirt *and* my backpack. I changed shirts, but I had to use his old backpack for a week."

Natasha's eyes widened. "Oh yeah—the Superman one, right?"

I laughed. "Batman, yeah. Believe me, I wasn't trying to make a fashion statement with that thing."

"Oh." Smiling, Natasha threw the paper towels away. "Anyway, it's not just the shirt. I completely forgot to do that essay for Spanish this weekend, so I was trying to write it on the bus. But I didn't finish it, and the stupid pen ruined what I wrote anyway, so I've got nothing to turn in. I've never gotten a zero on an assignment before."

"Spanish isn't till sixth period!" I said encouragingly. "You can do it during lunch. I'll help if you want."

Natasha looked surprised, but smiled. "Okay, thanks." We were both quiet for a few seconds, although it wasn't quite as awkward this time. Then she blurted out: "I'm really sorry about what happened at the band party. You know, with Aaron."

I stared at my shoes, feeling my cheeks redden. "It's okay. And I'm—I'm sorry about your shoes. You know, the spit valve. I, um . . . it wasn't an accident."

"Oh."

"It was so dumb, I can't believe I did that," I went on, unable to tear my gaze off the floor. "I mean, the whole thing with Aaron—I know you didn't *actually* do it on purpose, just to make me—"

"No, I did."

I looked up. Natasha's face was red, too, but she continued. "You were right. I was just flirting with him because I knew it would bother you. I . . ." Her eyes welled up with tears, and she blinked rapidly. "Ever since I met Julia, she's talked about you practically nonstop. I was really nervous about meeting you. I was really nervous about *everything*—my old school was a lot smaller than this one, the band was a *lot* smaller too, and . . . I don't know. It was kind of scary."

Swallowing, she reached for more paper towels. "You know that debate meet last week, during the pep rally? I totally bombed it. It was seriously awful. And then I forgot about this Spanish assignment . . . and I'm so nervous about the football game. I'll probably screw up the solo too, just like I've been screwing up everything else."

With a shaky sigh, she ran the towels under the faucet and wiped at her cheeks. I stared at her dumbly. All that know-it-all talk—Julia had been right. Natasha was just insecure.

It took me a few seconds to find my voice.

"You won't screw it up," I told her. "And even if you do, it won't be nearly as bad as me at the pep rally."

Natasha smiled. "Sophie told me about that. But you're really good, Holly. I'm sure it wasn't as bad as you think it was."

"Oh no," I said emphatically. "It. Was. *Bad*." We both laughed as the first bell rang.

Groaning, Natasha gestured to her shirt. "I can't believe I have to go around looking like this all day."

"Yeah, that—oh, wait a minute!" I exclaimed, unzipping my backpack. "Here, use this."

Natasha took my red hoodie, her eyes wide. "Seriously?"

"Yes, take it." I glanced down at her feet. "Sorry it doesn't go with your sandals, though."

She giggled, slipping the jacket on. "Yeah. Although it totally matches my bag!"

I grinned, watching her pick up the light blue backpack with red trim. "It does. Actually, I've got a lot of outfits that match it perfectly, especially this one top. That's the same bag I had that my brother ruined."

"Are you serious?" Natasha laughed again. "I guess we kind of have the same taste."

"Yup—*good* taste."

We stepped out into the crowded hall and looked at each other. "See you in band, I guess," I said.

"Okay. And thanks again for the hoodie," Natasha added.

"Anytime." I started to turn, then stopped. "Hey, I got the invitation. For your party Saturday."

"Oh, right." Natasha adjusted her backpack and smiled uncertainly. "I . . . I really hope you'll come. If you like these sandals, I've got another pair that would match that yellow dress you wore last week. We're probably the same size."

"Ooh, thanks!" I said excitedly. "And I'll bring that red top. Oh, and we've got the same boots, only mine are brown and yours are black—we can swap!"

"Yeah!" Natasha's eyes got big and round. "Wow. We could double our wardrobe."

I stared back at her. "Whoa, we could!"

"So . . . you're coming, then? To the party?"

I grinned. "I'll be there."

When I walked into English, Gabby stared at me. "What are you so happy about?" she asked around a mouthful of M&M's.

I shrugged, still smiling. "Nothing. Just having a good day so far."

Chapter Twenty-One

"I'm freaking out."

I watched Julia fumble to open her clarinet case. "You're going to do great," I assured her.

Kneeling, Julia opened her case and started putting her clarinet together. "Maybe. I mean, those cards definitely helped. But my whole grade in history depends on this test tomorrow. If I fail, my parents are going to flip."

"You *won't* fail," I insisted. "Look, you have no idea how lost I was in science the first few weeks. If I can pass that, I know you can pass history."

Julia smiled, but she still looked doubtful.

"Hey, guys."

We both glanced up at Natasha, holding her horn in one hand and my hoodie in the other. "Here you go, Holly," she said, handing it to me. "Thanks again for letting me use it yesterday."

"You're welcome." I couldn't help but notice Julia

was trying not to smile. "Julia's freaking out about the history test you guys have tomorrow," I informed Natasha. "Tell her to quit worrying."

"Quit worrying," Natasha said promptly, and Julia laughed. "Seriously, you'll be fine. Want to study after school today?"

Julia glanced at me. "Actually, um . . . Holly's coming over to help me. She made these cards, and—"

"You should come," I interrupted.

Julia and Natasha both looked at me in surprise.

"Really?" Natasha asked hesitantly.

I nodded. "Yeah, for sure."

After they headed into the band hall, I walked over to my cubby. When I turned around, horn in hand, Gabby was right behind me.

"You scared me!" I exclaimed. Gabby grinned, and I narrowed my eyes. "What?"

"Nothing," she said innocently. "Just that I heard you're coming to Natasha's party Saturday."

I raised my eyebrows. "So?"

"Sooo . . ." Gabby tilted her head. "I guess maybe Natasha isn't so bad after all, huh?"

I sighed. "Okay, fine. You were right; she's not so bad."

Gabby put her hand on her chest dramatically. "You have no idea how much I love being told I'm right," she said, and I giggled. "Hey, good luck on the chair test today."

"Thanks! You too."

By the time we finished with warm-ups, my stomach was tingling with nerves. But I wasn't nearly as nervous as I'd been for the first chair test. I still wanted to be first chair, of course. More than that, though, I just wanted to play my best.

Like last time, Mr. Dante started with the flutes and moved through the clarinets. I listened to each one, trying to hear what Mr. Dante heard. Who just played the notes, and who was "saying something."

I could definitely hear it with Gabby. The chorale just sounded different when she played it. When her turn ended, it was totally obvious she was the best out of everyone who'd gone so far.

Until Natasha played.

I closed my eyes, listening hard. Not for mistakes, like I had during the first chair test. I just listened.

Natasha really was great.

By the time she finished, I understood why Mr. Dante had given her first chair. The chorale was so not boring when she played. It was music.

When she finished, I leaned over as Mr. Dante scribbled a few notes.

"Nice job," I whispered.

Natasha smiled at me. "Thanks. Good luck!"

Mr. Dante set his pencil down. "Holly, go ahead."

Sitting up straight, I stared at the sheet music for a second. Then I closed my eyes and played.

I didn't miss a note or a rhythm, I played all the dynamics, I breathed in all the right places. It was actually the best I'd ever played it.

I wasn't sure if I sounded as good as Natasha had, or Gabby, for that matter. But I was pretty sure I could get there if I kept practicing.

𝄞

"Your turn, Natasha."

Brows furrowed, Natasha studied her cards. I leaned over to peer at Julia's hand.

"Okay . . . Santa Anna." Natasha tossed a card onto the bed, and we all giggled at the picture. (Seriously, drawing was *not* one of my talents. Santa Anna looked more like he was riding an anteater than a horse.)

Julia waved me away when I tried to peek at her cards again, chose one, and placed it on top of Natasha's. "The Alamo Mission!"

I flipped through her history textbook (even though I knew she was right). "Yup! And what happened at—"

"Battle of the Alamo, 1836, blah-blah-blah," Julia interrupted. "I got it." She put her remaining cards down and grinned at me. "I think you're right—I might actually pass!"

"Of course you will!" Natasha said, flipping one of her own cards over and grinning. "Oh my God, Holly. What is this supposed to be?" She held it up, and I tried to look offended.

"It's the Rio Grande. Duh."

Julia snorted. "It looks like a giant blue worm. See all the lines?"

"Those are *waves*," I said indignantly, and they both laughed. "Okay, I can't draw like Owen. So sue me."

Natasha grabbed the box of crackers at the foot of the bed and popped a few into her mouth. "What are you talking about?"

"Owen came up with this game," Julia explained, stacking the cards into a neat pile. "He made some cards for Holly to help her when she . . . uh . . ." She trailed off, then shot me an apologetic glance.

I shrugged. "I was failing science," I told Natasha. "Owen's my lab partner, so he helped me. Actually, I think I have those cards in my bag." Reaching over, I grabbed my backpack off the floor and rummaged in the front pocket. "Yup!"

I spread my science cards out on the bed, and Julia and Natasha leaned over. "He had trouble in history last year," I informed them. "So I borrowed those from him to help me make Julia's."

"Wow." Julia picked one up to study the picture closer. "You're right, he's really good."

"Yeah," Natasha agreed, then laughed. "Still, what a dork." Glancing at me, she blushed. "No, I mean, don't get me wrong—Owen's really nice! I like him a lot. But you've got to admit, this *is* pretty dorky."

She held up a card. I recognized the mouse in the wizard hat and grinned.

"Actually, I think he's really cool."

First period the next morning dragged on forever. When the bell finally rang, I hurried to Julia's history class. I spotted her and Natasha leaving, broke into a run, and nearly tripped over a boy kneeling down to tie his shoe. (In the middle of the hall. Seriously, sixth-graders can act dumb.)

"Julia!" They both whirled around, and I tried to catch my breath. "How'd you do?"

"Good, I think!" Julia said, but she looked anxious. "I mean, definitely better than my first test. I just hope it was good enough to pass."

"I thought you were going to ask Mr. Peterson if he'd grade it for you after class," I said.

"There wasn't enough time." Julia sighed.

"But he doesn't have a class third period," Natasha told me. "He said he'd do it then."

"So you'll know before band!" I exclaimed. Julia smiled nervously.

"Yup."

I barely made it to PE on time. It was dodgeball day, and as it turned out, being distracted during a dodgeball game because your best friend was about to get either some very good or very bad news was *not* ideal. By the time I got to the band hall, I had more than a few bruises forming on my legs and arms.

Almost everyone was crowded around Mr. Dante's door, reading the paper posted there—chair test results. I stood on my tiptoes, scanning all the faces. No Julia. Turning, I hurried into the cubby room.

There she was, getting her clarinet case out. Next to her, Natasha was talking animatedly. When she saw me, she beamed.

"Holly, she passed!" Then she clapped both her hands over her mouth and glanced at Julia, who just laughed.

"You did?" I squealed, hopping up and down with excitement. Julia grinned.

"I got an eighty-eight!" she exclaimed. "Can you believe it?"

I tried to look exasperated, but it didn't really work since I couldn't stop smiling. "Well, *duh*. It was pretty obvious yesterday when you kicked Natasha's butt."

"Hey!" Natasha punched me lightly on the shoulder. "I didn't do *that* bad. And I have to admit, that game was pretty helpful."

"Yeah," Julia agreed. "Thanks again for making those, Holly."

I shrugged. "Anytime. And it wasn't my idea. You should tell—"

"Owen!" Natasha yelled. Turning, I saw Owen frozen in front of his cubby. Judging by the rapid blinking, he was rather alarmed to have the three of us staring at him.

"Yeah?"

"That game you made is really cool," Natasha said.

Julia nodded. "It helped me get a B in history," she added.

Owen looked relieved. "Oh good!" He smiled at me. "So you made some history cards, then?"

"Yup."

"Except hers are . . ." Natasha trailed off, giggling. Julia pulled the cards out of her backpack and handed them to Owen with a grin.

"Holly's not exactly an artist," she said, and I rolled my eyes.

Owen flipped through a few cards, then stopped on the Santa-Anna-riding-an-anteater card, eyebrows raised.

"Look," I said, glaring around at them. "I never said I was good at drawing."

After I got my horn out, we headed into the band hall. It wasn't until I sat down between Natasha and Brooke that I realized I'd never even looked at the chair test results. Half-standing out of my chair, I squinted, trying to read the list.

"Our section's the same," Natasha said. I gave her a

reassuring smile as I sat down again.

"I figured."

She relaxed a little. "Really? I wasn't so sure. You sounded awesome yesterday."

"So did you. Besides," I added teasingly, "I've got the rest of the year. You'd better keep practicing."

Natasha grinned. "You too."

𝄞

"Let's see—you've got your phone?"

I hopped from one foot to the other, one hand on the car door, the other tugging down my bright red band shirt. "Yes, Mom."

"What time is the game over?"

"Mr. Dante said probably eight, but I'll text you."

"And who's taking you to Spins?"

I sighed loudly. "Julia's dad is taking us."

"Got it."

Next to her, Dad leaned over from the driver's seat. "We'll try to sit as close to the band as we can, okay, sweetie?"

"You're not going to yell my name and wave every ten seconds like you do to Chad at his baseball games, are you?"

"No promises," Dad replied solemnly. I groaned, turning to leave.

Mom raised an eyebrow. "Holly, are you *sure* you have everything?"

"Mom!" I yelled, glancing over my shoulder. Two

other red shirts caught my eye; Gabby and Victoria were heading into the stadium. "Yes, okay? I'm going to be late!"

As soon as I shut the car door and started to hurry after Gabby, Mom rolled down the window. "Holly!"

Exasperated, I turned around. Mom held my French horn case up and gave me a Look.

Okay, maybe I was a *little* distracted.

Horn case in hand, I sprinted into the stadium and found the cluster of red shirts on the far right side. I took the stairs two at a time, squeezed past the saxophones, and plopped down on the bench next to Natasha. Mr. Dante hadn't even started taking role yet.

"Hey!" Natasha said, then glanced down. "Okay, those are *so* cool."

I grinned and wiggled my feet, which were wearing white high-tops with sparkly red laces. "Thanks!"

We spent most of the first quarter of the game talking about her birthday party the next day. (Mom had taken me shopping Thursday after school, and I got Natasha a mint-green belt that matched her sandals. I so could not wait to borrow both.) Then we spent the second quarter watching Aaron when he was on the field and making goofy faces at Julia when she'd turn around.

Of course, we played a lot, too. Every time our team scored, Mr. Dante leaped up and everyone grabbed his or her instrument for the fight song. And every time I heard the trumpet fanfare in the beginning, I thought about Aaron's valve getting stuck and giggled.

At halftime, Julia and Natasha and I went to buy drinks.

"Okay, I changed my mind." Natasha looked at me seriously. "You play the solo. I don't want to. I'm nervous."

I rolled my eyes. "Galactic March" was the first song we were supposed to play at the end of halftime.

"Nope. I already embarrassed myself once, thank you."

Natasha groaned. "I'm going to screw it up."

"No, you won't," Julia and I said simultaneously.

When we got back to the stands, a booming voice over the loudspeaker introduced the cheerleaders, who flipped and cartwheeled onto the field. I glanced around the stadium during their routine; most of the crowd had settled into their seats again. Sure enough, Mom and Dad had moved over to the section right next to the band. They waved at me frantically, and I waved back.

Then I saw Aaron running up the steps toward us, still in his football uniform. Great. Now I had to figure out how to play while hyperventilating. It got worse when his knee bumped into my back as he hurried to his spot.

"Sorry, Holly."

"It's okay," I squeaked, unable to look up at him. Natasha snickered.

When the cheerleaders ran off the field, the

loudspeaker voice boomed out again.

"And now, the Millican Middle School Band, performing 'Galactic March'!"

The crowd applauded, and Mr. Dante raised his arms. Natasha wasn't laughing anymore. Actually, she looked kind of pale.

We started to play. I tried to concentrate on the music, but I kept thinking about the pep rally. As the solo got closer and closer, my stomach started to tense. I tried to send Natasha a mental message. *Don't freak out like I did.*

I tapped my foot, counting the measures. Only three more. Two. One.

The whole band paused, and Natasha played.

She didn't freak out. She sounded *awesome.*

I couldn't stop smiling through the whole solo. In fact, I almost missed my entrance. When the march ended, I grabbed Natasha's arm and shook it excitedly.

"That was great!" I yelled over the cheering crowd, and she beamed.

"Thanks!"

When the third quarter started, Brooke and Owen switched places so she could talk to Laurie, one of the trombonists. Trevor slid down so he was right behind Owen, and a few seconds later, Warlock cards were spread out on the stands.

"Okay," Natasha whispered in my ear. "Now *that* is dorky."

I giggled. "It's actually a pretty fun game."

Her eyebrows arched. "You've played it?"

"Yup."

"No way."

Grinning, I turned around in my seat. "Trevor," I said solemnly, "tell Natasha about the time I totally destroyed you at this game."

Trevor scowled, and Owen burst out laughing.

They only got to play for about five minutes before our team scored and we had to play the fight song. Then there was a field goal, and we played the fight song again. Two minutes later we scored another touchdown and Owen sighed, stacking the cards and shoving them into his pocket before grabbing his horn.

"I give up."

But half of the fourth quarter passed with neither team scoring. I glanced at the scoreboard; we were still winning by fourteen. Next to me, Natasha and Gabby were deep in conversation. On my other side, Owen doodled in a notebook.

No, wait—a sketchbook. I watched his pencil fly over the paper, fascinated. He really was good.

"Wow."

Pausing, Owen glanced at me in surprise.

"Sorry, that's just—that's really awesome." I leaned in closer, studying the picture. "How many drawings do you have, anyway?"

Turning the sketchbook sideways, Owen flipped through the pages. "I've got six more books at home. So kind of a lot, I guess."

Kind of? I thought. Then something caught my eye. "Hang on—what's that?"

I stared at the page he'd stopped on. It was divided into a neat grid; six squares across, three down. Each one had a different sketch, but no color. They looked kind of familiar.

"These are like the cards you made for science," I said, and he nodded.

"Yup."

I gazed at them. It had taken me a whole Saturday afternoon to make my lame cards for Julia. Owen must have spent tons and tons of time on those cards for me.

"Why didn't you use these?"

"They're for the next unit," he explained.

I stared at him. "Huh?"

"We're starting a new unit next week," Owen said. "They're almost done, I just need to color them." He looked confused, probably because I was still staring at him. "What?"

I blinked, then looked back at the sketchbook. "Nothing! I just—I didn't know you were making more."

"Well, yeah . . . oh." His face fell. "I guess maybe you don't need help anymore, do you?"

"No, I do!" I said immediately. "And I still want to hang out after school. I mean, I have a bet to win. *Cyborgs versus Ninjas*, right?"

Owen grinned. "Right."

I glanced back at the pictures. "But seriously, this is like . . . a whole lot of work."

He shrugged. "I guess. It's fun, though."

"Yeah." Smiling, I handed him the sketchbook. "Thanks for doing it."

Mr. Dante stood up. "Get ready for the fight song!" he called. Glancing at the scoreboard, I realized there were only a few seconds left in the game.

As the clock ran down, the cheers grew louder. Someone bumped into my back, and I glanced over my shoulder.

"Sorry again," Aaron said with a grin.

"It's okay!" I didn't squeak this time, which was an improvement. "Hey, I thought you went back down there after halftime!"

"I did," he replied. "But I was on the bench most of fourth quarter, and Coach said I could come up here."

"Fight song!" Mr. Dante called again, and Aaron lifted his trumpet.

"Any stuck valves?" I said teasingly. He laughed, making a show of pressing each one.

"Nope! All good."

Grinning, I faced front again and realized Natasha and Gabby were watching me and giggling. Gabby gave me a little thumbs-up, and I pressed my lips together so I wouldn't laugh.

Outside the stadium, Julia, Natasha, and I waited for Mr. Gordon to pick us up. My parents passed us in their car, waving out the windows. Rolling my eyes, I waved back.

"You guys are going to Spins, right?" Gabby joined

us, holding a newly opened box of Red Hots.

"Yup! Are you?" I asked.

"Let's see . . . pepperoni pizza, or my mom's leftover cabbage soup?" Gabby tilted her head, pretending to consider it. "Yeah, I'm coming."

We laughed, and then Natasha let out a little cry.

"Here comes Aaron," she hissed, nudging me. "Ask him to come."

"What? No!" I hissed back, toying with my turtle necklace. (Julia and I had found a dolphin one online and ordered it for Natasha's birthday so we could all match.)

"Come on, just do it!" Julia whispered. "A bunch of people are going; it's not just us."

"No. No way."

"Holly," Natasha whined. "Just do it. Do it do it do it—"

"Oh, for the love . . ." Rolling her eyes, Gabby poked Aaron in the arm with her saxophone as he passed us. "Hey, we're going to Spins. Want to come?"

I wanted to disappear right on the spot. Not because Gabby invited him, but because Julia and Natasha were looking at me and giggling and my face was burning and oh my God it was all just so. Totally. Obvious.

But Aaron just grinned. "Sure! I'll be there."

Thankfully, Gabby waited until he was out of earshot before turning to me with a satisfied smirk. "You're welcome," she said, popping a few Red Hots into her mouth. I tried to look mad and failed, mostly because I couldn't stop smiling like an idiot.

"There's my dad!" Julia said, and I saw Mr. Gordon's little blue Honda pull up to the curb. "Bye, Gabby!"

"See you in a few minutes!" Gabby waved as we ran toward the parking lot. Julia opened the trunk and we tossed our cases inside. Opening the back door, I slid into the middle seat, and Julia plopped down next to me. Natasha squeezed in on my other side and shut the door, and Mr. Gordon glanced at us in the rearview mirror.

"What, no one wants to sit up front with me?"

"Nope!" Julia said, laughing.

Mr. Gordon grinned at me. "Are you all right in the middle there? You're looking kind of . . . squished."

I shrieked as Julia and Natasha squeezed me in on either side. "I'm good!" I managed to gasp out between giggles.

He laughed. "If you say so."

They were still trying to tickle me as we pulled out of the stadium parking lot and headed to Spins, but I didn't mind being in the middle one bit.

Acknowledgments

First, a huge thank-you to my editor and fellow band geek, Jordan Hamessley—the only person in the publishing industry I've met who loves sharing stories about halftime shows, spit-valve mishaps, and which Texas marching band won state a decade ago as much as I do. And an equally huge thanks to Sarah Fabiny for taking a chance on me with this series.

To my agent and fellow musician, Sarah Davies, for years of constant support, advice, and encouragement. (I hate to publicly blow her cover, but she's actually Superwoman.)

To art director and designer extraordinaires Giuseppe Castellano and Mallory Grigg for the mind-boggling amount of work they put into this series, and for letting me be involved in the incredible process. And to illustrator Genevieve Kote, whose work really is pitch-perfect.

To four of the most talented writers and supportive friends I've ever known—Amanda Hannah, Kate Hart, Kirsten Hubbard, and Kaitlin Ward—for the critiques, the encouragement, the snark, the random, the fursplosions, the pep talks, the inspiration, and on and on and on.

To my parents, John and Mary, and my sister, Heather—to say you've been supportive just doesn't do it justice. Maybe it's better to say thank you for not thinking I'm completely insane . . . or if you did think so, thank you for not saying it.

To Josh, for playing music with me, running around the world with me, and encouraging me when I decided to try telling stories for a living. And to Adi, for being the best lab assistant ever.

Lastly, to every band geek I taught, taught with, or was taught by—thank you. Also, the characters in this book are fictional and are not based on any of you. Mostly.

Be sure to pick up

Turn the page for a sneak peek!

Winning isn't everything.

I tell myself that a lot. Sometimes I believe it, too.

Like with friendships—that's a red light. Getting too competitive with a friend is a good way to make an enemy.

Then there's stuff like band—yellow light. Proceed with caution. Winning is great, but it's not the only thing that matters.

And then there's video games, like *Prophet Wars*—major green light. It's total galaxy-wide domination or go home.

The problem is, *everything's* a green light for me, at least at first. It's like an instinct. That's why, when my band director decided to make our fund-raiser a competition, my first thought was that my bandmates were going down like an alien airship flying over my level-three jungle subterranean missile silo.

What? Maybe winning isn't everything, but it's still pretty awesome.

It was fourth period at Millican Middle School, which meant I was in the band hall for advanced band rehearsal. Last week, Mr. Dante had announced that we would be going to New Orleans for a band contest in March. And *that* meant four days of staying up late in hotel rooms, competing at a big band contest at an amusement park, and missing classes. To help pay for the trip, the band was going to hold a bake sale.

Mr. Dante pushed his glasses up his nose and looked around the band hall. "As some of you might know, our girls' volleyball team is in the playoffs," he said. "Three of their tournaments are going to be held in our gym, and Coach Reyes has agreed to allow us to sell concessions during the games. We're going to split into teams—woodwind, brass, and percussion." He held up a finger when Derrick Adler raised his hand from where he stood behind a xylophone.

"Don't worry," Mr. Dante said. "I'm aware that this isn't an even match as far as how many students are on each team. That's why I'm not judging this by the total amount of money you make. Instead, the winning section will be the one that averages the most money raised per student. The important thing here is that you work together as a team."

On my right, Natasha Prynne raised her hand. "What does the winning section get?" she asked, and I couldn't help but grin. Natasha was pretty much as competitive as me, which was why she sat next to me as first chair in our section. She was also one of my best friends. (See? I could handle not winning. Sometimes.)

"Glad you asked," Mr. Dante said, smiling. "The section that wins will actually get two prizes. First, they'll get to decide on the final design for the new T-shirts I'm going to order for our trip to New Orleans."

Trevor Wells's hand shot up. "You mean like we can pick any design at all?" he asked. I rolled my eyes. Knowing Trevor, he was probably picturing us in band T-shirts covered in wizards or dragons or something equally lame.

“Within reason,” Mr. Dante told him. “As for the other prize . . .” He cleared his throat. “At my last school, I had a tradition of dressing as Santa to conduct the advanced band at the winter concert.”

“Santa?” Gabby Flores said in disbelief, then caught herself and raised her hand. Mr. Dante nodded at her. “Santa?” she repeated, and several kids giggled. “Are you serious? Why?”

“Because I’m a jolly person,” Mr. Dante said with a perfectly straight face. Now I was laughing, too.

Mr. Dante looked a little miffed. “Anyway, I thought maybe I could start a new tradition here at Millican. I’ll still dress as Santa at the winter concert, but the winning section can choose to alter or add to my costume however they’d like.” He paused. “Again, within reason.”

A voice behind me caused my stomach to flutter. “You mean, we could make you zombie Santa?” asked Aaron Cook, and several students laughed.

“That’s the idea,” Mr. Dante replied. “But—”

“Vampire Santa!” exclaimed Sophie Wheeler.

Gabby grinned. “Hippie Santa!”

My best friend, Julia Gordon, caught my eye from the clarinet section. “How about *Mrs.* Claus?” she called with a wicked grin, and everyone cracked up.

Mr. Dante held his hands up, but he was smiling, too. “Whatever the costume, it has to be approved by the band boosters. And speaking of,” he added, holding up a stack of papers, “I need you all to take these home to your parents. We’ll need a few of them to volunteer, both at the volleyball games and with any baking your section does."

Natasha leaned closer to me as he passed out the papers. "Not good. I tried baking cookies once—we ended up feeding them to the neighbor's dog," she whispered, and I grinned.

"Hang on, I've got an idea." After making sure Mr. Dante was still handing out papers, I leaned back and reached behind Brooke Dennis, tapping Owen Reynolds on the shoulder.

Owen was fourth-chair horn. His real talent was drawing. Well, that and *Prophets*. We hung out at his house every Thursday afternoon to blow up virtual aliens. Last week, his mom had made us these amazing cream-cheese brownies to celebrate that we finally got to level four.

"Do you think your mom could help us?" I asked softly. "Those brownies, maybe?"

Owen nodded. "I'll ask her."

Smiling, I turned back to Natasha. "Owen's mom will help us. I know she'll say yes."

"Cool," said Natasha. "Hey, how are you doing on the all-region music?"

Wrinkling my nose, I pulled Fugue in F Minor out of my folder and set it on my music stand. "Not bad. I'm still having trouble near the end, right here," I said, pointing.

Natasha nodded. "Yeah, that part's really hard. Want to work on it together sometime?"

Mr. Dante was getting back up on the podium, so I just nodded in response. All-region auditions were in a few weeks. Band students from all seven middle schools in the Oak Point School District could audition to be in one of the two all-region bands. In February, they'd get to miss an entire day of school to go to rehearsal with a guest conductor, and then they'd perform at a concert.

Two bands meant a total of eight French horn spots, and who knew how many horn players in the district would be auditioning. It would be tough to make it, but Natasha and I were going to try. Especially since Mr. Dante had decided that the all-region results would count as our next chair test.

Natasha grabbed her pencil and scrawled something on the bottom of my étude.

Tomorrow after school?

I gave her a thumbs-up.

While Mr. Dante tuned the flutes one at a time, I studied the étude, tapping my fingers. Natasha was an amazing horn player and a good friend, but all-region was a yellow light, and I was going to do my best to make it.

"I swear, Holly, I'm still having nightmares."

I pressed my lips together to keep from laughing. Julia glared at me.

"I'm serious!" she cried. "You said it wouldn't be that scary."

"No, I said it wouldn't be that *gory*," I replied, grinning. Last weekend for Halloween, my brother Chad and I went to the Asylum—ranked the third-best haunted house in Austin. And since he was meeting a bunch of his friends there, I'd convinced him to let me bring Julia and Natasha, too.

Or maybe *drag* would be a better word.

"The worst part was the clowns," Julia said, shuddering as we skirted around a group of eighth-grade girls and headed into C-hall.

"Really?" I asked. "I thought the scariest part was when we were crammed in that tiny room and the guy crawled across the ceiling."

Julia stopped, her eyes round. "What?"

"You don't remember?"

She started walking again, brow furrowed. "I remember the tiny room, and I remember the scratching noises. But I had my eyes closed."

I smiled. "That's probably a good thing."

"Someone *crawled across the ceiling*? Over our *heads*?" I didn't respond, and Julia groaned. "Never again, Holly. Seriously."

A flyer on the wall right outside the computer lab caught my eye. "Hey, look!" I grabbed Julia's arm and pointed.

"Oh yeah, the winter dance!" she exclaimed. "I totally forgot to tell you, I saw them putting up flyers in the gym today, too."

"Really?" I gave her an innocent look as we headed

to our computers. "During PE?"

Julia rolled her eyes, blushing. "Yes, during PE. And no, I didn't talk to Seth."

I pressed the power button on my computer, then swiveled my chair around to face Julia. "You should ask him to the dance."

She snorted. "Yeah, right."

"I'm serious!" I insisted. "He likes you, Julia. But he's so shy, he'll never ask."

I didn't know Seth Anderson really well. We had math together in sixth grade, but he hardly ever talked. All I knew about him was that he played cello in the orchestra and he couldn't say hi to my best friend without stammering.

Julia shook her head as she typed in her password. "Probably. But that doesn't make it any easier for me to ask him."

"What's so hard?" I said. "'Hey, Seth, would you go to the winter dance with me?' Done."

Julia gave me a withering look. "Okay, if it's so easy, why don't you do it?"

I blinked. "Ask Seth to the dance for you? That's—"

"No!" Julia interrupted, laughing. "I mean ask Aaron, you dork."

Now it was my turn to blush. I'd had a crush on Aaron since the first day of seventh grade. Okay, fine, since last year. But it was still a huge accomplishment when I managed to talk to him without turning tomato red. That was his fault, though. Him and his dark brown eyes. And his smile with the creases like parentheses in his cheeks. And his—

"Hello?" Julia waved her hand in front of my face, giggling when I jumped. "So, yes or no?"

"Yes or no what?"

"You know what. Will you ask him?" She arched an eyebrow. "Since it's so easy and all."

Ugh. She was right—the thought of asking Aaron to the winter dance made me kind of nauseated.

But a tiny part of me was excited at the thought, too. I tapped my fingers on the arm of my chair.

"The dance isn't till December," I said, thinking out loud. "It's too early to ask anyone."

"True."

"So how's this," I went on. "We make a pact."

"Why do I get the feeling I'm not going to like this?" Julia closed her eyes like she was bracing herself.

"We wait till Thanksgiving break," I said. "If Seth hasn't asked you, you'll ask him. Same with me and Aaron. Deal?"

Julia squinted at me with one eye. "You're serious, aren't you?"

"Come on!" I said encouragingly. "Thanksgiving's not for a month. Plenty of time to prepare."

"You'll really do it, though?" Julia asked. "If I ask Seth to the dance, you'll ask Aaron?"

I smiled, ignoring the butterflies flapping around my stomach. "Yeah, I'll do it."

"Okay." Julia grinned at me. "It's a deal."

About the Author

Michelle Schusterman is a former band director and forever band geek, starting back in the sixth grade when she first picked up a pair of drumsticks. Now she writes books, screenplays, and music in New York City, where she lives with her husband (and bandmate) and their chocolate Lab (who is more of a vocalist).